CW00867206

Baked with Love

Lily McDermott Series Book 2

ABOUT THE AUTHOR

Izzy Bayliss lives in Ireland with her husband, children, and their dog. A romantic at heart, she loves nothing more than cosying up in front of the fire with a good book. Her motto is that reality is overrated and she is happiest staring into space and daydreaming. She released The Girl I Was Before in 2016 and its sequel Baked with Love in 2018.

You can find out more about Izzy Bayliss on www.izzybayliss.com.
She can also be found hanging about on Facebook @izzybaylissauthor or Twitter @izzybayliss.

If you would like to be the first to hear about Izzy's latest releases and other news then please subscribe to her newsletter on www.izzybayliss.com – she promises not to spam you!

This novel is entirely a work of fiction. The names, characters, and incidents portrayed in it are the work of the author's imagination. Any resemblance to actual persons, living or deceased, events or localities is purely coincidental.

http://www.izzybayliss.com

PRAISE FOR
'The Girl I was Before'

"A brilliant new Irish author"
Kelly Spillane, Kelly Reads Books

"A curl up on the sofa and eat chocolate kind of book"
Kaisha Holloway, The Writing Garnet

For Simon – for everything

I'm always telling people that cake has magical powers. Everyone knows that feeling when a buttery sponge melts on your tongue and suddenly a bad day is set to right. Or the moment you bite into a lighter than air pastry, flakes falling down around you, and the problems in your life are temporarily suspended. A slice of cake can be five minutes of magic in the middle of a chaotic day. A thick chocolate ganache is a heavenly balm for a crisis of the heart, while the crunch of a meringue on a fine summer's day can make us feel warm inside. Cake is food for the soul and each little bite you take is a little piece of enchantment. And if you don't believe me, then let me show you .

. .

* * *

CHAPTER 1

Can't breathe . . . can't breathe . . . can't breeeeathe . . .

"Ehm, Lily, why is your face turning purple?" Sam asked, his face a mixture of concern and amusement.

I was looking at my reflection in the glass and sucking my stomach in so much that I thought I was going to starve my brain of oxygen. I exhaled and let everything hang out again. It was useless; I'd never be able to keep that up all night.

I was standing in my newly appointed *Baked with Love* and it was a few minutes before the first guests were due to arrive for the launch party. I couldn't believe that I was about to open my very own bakery – me, Lily McDermott, a bakery owner? It sounded ridiculous even to me.

"Are you sure I look okay?" I said, turning around to him.

"You look great, Lily – I've told you a million times already!"

"I don't look like a person who should have their own bakery though, do I?" Although I had had my hair blow-dried and I had bought a gorgeous new tea dress, the nerves were starting to get the better of me. Whenever I looked at my reflection in the mirror, I didn't look mature enough to own my own business. I felt like an imposter.

"What are you talking about?" Sam asked with a laugh.

"Me . . . this –" I said, gesturing around the café with a sigh. "Oh God, I think I'm in over my head . . ." You know when for once everything in your life is going right and you finally think you have your act together? Nope, me neither because here I was yet again in a situation where I felt totally out of my depth.

My best friend, Frankie, had invited lots of journalists and PR people and I knew they would be expecting somebody confident, somebody assured, somebody who knew what they were doing, not someone who was completely winging it. I felt like this was all a big charade. I was waiting for somebody to jump out and say, "Haha, Lily, you didn't really think we were going to let you open your own bakery, did you?"

"Relax, Lily, it'll be great!" Sam reassured me, taking me into his arms.

"But what if nobody turns up?" I said for possibly the hundred and seventh time that day.

"Well, then me and you will have a lot of cake to get through –"

I glared at him. "That's not even funny!"

He grinned back at me. "Lily, stop fretting, of course they will. You've had loads of RSVPs. You've worked hard for this, try to relax and enjoy your special moment."

"You're right." I sighed, wondering once again why I had decided to do this. Was I completely mad?

As I looked around the room, I couldn't believe that this place was mine. A wooden sign with *Baked with Love* now hung proudly over the door and the fringe of a huge red and white candy-striped awning billowed gently underneath. In good weather, I would be able to put a few tables under it. The original oak floorboards were still intact, and two old bottle glass windows looked out onto Bluebell Lane where inside I had created a tower of macarons to entice people through the door. A traditional style glass counter ran along one wall, which was now full with cakes and treats. I had an old-fashioned, push-button till at the end of the counter. A comfy sofa ran along the back wall beside the gas stove which I hoped would give the place a warm, cosy feel during the long winter months. The room at the back was fitted out as my kitchen, and I was so excited to have proper catering ovens, an industrial-size fridge, and tonnes of space to work. I felt like a child at Christmas over the last few days as I tested out the new equipment. I would be able to double, if not treble, my output every day. I had bought some mismatched tables and chairs which, as well as being cheaply purchased in the charity shop, gave the place a relaxed and welcoming feel. I had also picked up vintage-patterned plates and teacups, saucers and bowls; none were from the same set but somehow, collectively, they all worked together. The end result was that *Baked with Love* was cute and homely and exactly what I had imagined my dream bakery might look like way back when I had been working out of my kitchen in Ballyrobin.

I had viewed unit after unit over the past few months, but inevitably they were too small, or too big, or didn't have space for a kitchen, or were on the quiet end of the street. Every place I had looked at hadn't been right, but this little shop was just perfect. I could feel it in my bones.

I would be eternally grateful to my brother-in-law, Tom,

11

who had a large property portfolio around Dublin and was cutting me a deal on the unit. The previous tenants had only vacated the building recently, and Tom had said it was mine if I wanted it. There wasn't a chance I could ever hope to afford the rent on a prime location like Bluebell Lane without his help. I turned back around and looked around the room and once more a nervous feeling began bubbling its way up inside me.

It wasn't long before my Dad and Frankie came through the door, followed shortly by my sister, Clara, and her husband, Tom. I was relieved to see Clara hadn't brought her boys, Jacob and Joshua, with her. I had visions of my brand-new bakery being destroyed by her "energetic" sons. Frankie arrived next wearing an electric blue coat over a cerise pink dress. Most people with Frankie's pale colouring and wiry auburn hair would shy away from wearing bright colours but not her. Her job as a freelance fashion stylist meant she wasn't afraid to experiment with clothes.

"Are you ready?" she asked, kissing me on both cheeks.

"Do you think anyone would notice if I ran away right now?"

"Don't worry, you'll be great," she said, giving me a squeeze.

Soon the rest of the guests began to arrive, and I watched in amazement as Frankie turned into my PR woman. She had invited Ireland's top journalists and food bloggers and other people who she said were social media "influencers" – whatever they were. She confidently greeted people and introduced them to me until my head was spinning trying to keep up with who was who.

Frankie had insisted that we needed a theme, so we were simply going with "Cake and Cocktails." We had designed strawberry mojitos to complement the Eton-mess, which were served in a shot glass alongside the cocktail. There were sticky toffee apple martinis to match my bite-sized sticky toffee puddings, and Frankie had suggested gin-gin mules to pair with the key lime cupcakes. Dad and Sam had been given the job of serving the guests, and Frankie directed them through the crowd with their trays so that everyone had a drink and matching cake in their hands.

I was so busy running around meeting and greeting the journalists and PR people that Frankie was introducing me to and trying to make a good impression that before I knew it she was tipping a spoon against the side of a wine glass calling on me to make a speech. My stomach flipped over; I had been dreading this bit. I managed to catch Sam's eye across the room, and he gave me a reassuring wink.

I swallowed back a lump in my throat and began. My voice trembled with emotion when I gave a special mention to Frankie for encouraging me to set up my own cake-making business in the first place. It was hard to believe that an idea that was conceived over a bottle of wine one night was now almost a fully fledged bakery. I could never have imagined when I first took those tentative steps into business that I would one day have a café with my name over the door. To see *Baked with Love*, my own bakery, alive with people eating and chatting and laughing was everything I had ever dreamed of. I finished by

13

saying: "Thank you, everyone, for coming, I think we have the recipe for a perfect night: a great crowd, some lovely cocktails, and hopefully some tasty treats."

The rest of the night went past in a blur, and before I knew it I was saying goodbye to everyone as they assured me that they would be giving *Baked with Love* a big thumbs up.

As soon as we had closed the door on the last guest, I let out a huge sigh of relief and collapsed onto a chair.

"I think it was a success!" Sam said, coming over and wrapping me into a hug.

"I don't think I said anything too stupid . . ."

"You need to work on your public speaking, but otherwise I think people actually enjoyed it," Clara said.

"Of course they did!" Frankie said, cutting across her. She had no patience for Clara's antics.

"I'm proud of you, Lily," Dad said.

After we were finished cleaning up, Frankie, Dad, Clara, and Tom headed on leaving just Sam and me alone together.

"You were amazing tonight," he said, taking me into his arms. "Come on, this calls for some bubbles!" He took me by the hand. We locked up and stepped out onto the pedestrianised street where the aprons of cafés and bars fronted. Office workers walked past us, blazers draped over their shoulders and ties loosened on the warm evening.

We walked over to a nearby bar and took a seat outside under the canopy. Sam disappeared inside and returned a few moments later with a bottle of champagne. He uncorked it and the froth rushed over the neck and down onto the table. He poured us both a glass.

"To *Baked with Love*," he toasted.

"To *Baked with Love*," I echoed.

He put his arm around my shoulder, and we sat back and watched the busy street life unfold before us.

"I never thought I'd say it but my life it pretty perfect right now, Sam Waters." I reached for his hand and gave it a squeeze. When I thought back over how things had gone for the last two years, a whirlwind didn't even begin to describe it. In that period, I had married Marc and separated. I had been fired from my job in Rapid Response pregnancy tests and had set up *Baked with Love* from my own kitchen. I had met Sam when he had come to my rescue after a disaster involving a stand of fallen cupcakes and my nephews, Jacob and Joshua. After a few false starts, we had finally got it together and now here I was, relaxing in his strong arms, looking across the street at my new bakery. I almost had to pinch myself to believe it was true. From one of the lowest points of my life, all these good things had happened to me and it was all because of the magic of cake.

It was then that I noticed Sam lowering his gaze towards the cobblestones on the ground.

"What is it?" I asked.

"It's nothing – sorry . . ." He smiled at me and squeezed my hand.

We sat chatting and people watching and staring across at *Baked with Love* with a mixture of pride and amazement until the cool evening air began to make its presence felt. I began to shiver, and Sam took his jacket off the back of the chair and draped it over my shoulders.

After we had finished the bottle we strolled home hand in hand along the Grand Canal towards Sam's apartment. It had become my apartment too over the last year. He had let me take over his kitchen with my baking on the condition that I saved him some of whatever I had made that day. I figured it was a win-win for both of us, so I had put my house in Ballyrobin up for rent and moved in with Sam the very next day.

I felt as though I was dancing on air the whole way home. The sun began to set in shades of pink and orange over the Grand Canal basin, glinting off the water below and bedding down somewhere over Boland's Mill. Dublin really could be the best city in the world on a sunny evening like this, I thought.

When we reached the apartment, I walked over to the floor-to-ceiling length windows. Dusk had started to fall, and a field of city lights lay twinkling beyond the pane. I drew the curtains across and flopped down onto the red L-shaped sofa that ran the length of the wall.

Sam sat down beside me and took me into his arms.

"I'm proud of you. I know you'll make it a success."

"I hope so," I said, nervously biting down on my bottom lip.

"You make me so happy, you know that don't you, Lily?" he said suddenly.

I smiled and looked up at Sam's handsome face, the cutting cheekbones dotted with dark stubble. But he wasn't smiling; instead, his face had clouded over. His brow was furrowed downwards emphasising the crease above the bridge of his nose.

I was taken aback by his serious expression. "I know that, Sam, I love you too." I laughed to try and lighten the situation, but I noticed that he wasn't meeting my eyes. A cold feeling washed over me and I didn't like it one bit. It was unsettling. I had been here before.

Suddenly, his face relaxed and his mouth broke into a grin and I relaxed then too. There was something about his smile that always seemed to calm even the worst of my neuroses. I was just imagining it; everything was fine.

CHAPTER 2

The next morning, I opened my eyes and let them adjust to the dusky half-light of the room. I had barely slept. I had spent most of the night staring at the shadows cast by the streetlights as they crept across the ceiling, my mind racing with plans for *Baked with Love*.

The room was filled with the noise of the city coming to life below me. I could hear the sound of tooting cars as traffic began to fill the streets and the beeping of a reversing bin lorry. The list of things that I needed to do for *Baked with Love* kept spinning around in my head. Sam was still sleeping soundly, so I pulled back the duvet and climbed out of bed. I was so bloody nervous. Today was the day I was throwing open the doors of my bakery for the whole world to see. There was no going back now. All my hopes and dreams for the last few months had finally come true; I just hoped it would be a success. Dad was going to give me a hand behind the counter, and Clara had offered her help as well. If it got busy all I had to do was give her a call and she would leave the boys with Olga, her latest in a string of long-suffering au pairs. I wasn't too keen on taking her up on it though. She'd probably scare away any customers that I did manage to get.

I dressed in a bright pink tea dress with a black rose pattern and well-worn, flat Roman sandals because I knew I would be running around on my feet all day. I tied my hair up into a bun and quickly did my make-up. I kissed a sleeping Sam a swift goodbye, then I climbed onto my bike and cycled over the cobbled streets of Dublin until I reached Bluebell Lane.

As I came upon my bakery, I almost had to pinch myself. It looked so pretty under the watery morning sun. I parked my bike on a nearby lamp post and then with pride I walked over, took the key out of my pocket, twisted it in the lock, and pushed open the door. The bell gave its pleasing little trrring. How I loved that sound.

As I surveyed the room, I felt like a proper grown-up. I couldn't believe somebody had entrusted me, Lily McDermott, with my own building. Sometimes I felt totally overwhelmed by the responsibility of it all that I could barely breathe. My chest tightened and my heart started rattling. Be cool, I told myself, you've got this.

I went into the kitchen and immediately fired up the ovens. I looked around the room where glass jars ran along my shelves filled with jams, flavourings, and decorations. The fridge was full of catering tubs of butter and bottles of cream. Trays of free-range eggs sourced from an organic farm in County Kildare that were so fresh that some still had feathers stuck to them, sat on the worktops. I had everything prepared and ready to go. I set to making scones, lovingly combining the ingredients into a soft dough, and once I had them loaded in the oven, I bent down to the chalkboard and wrote in curly script:

'Good morning from *Baked with Love*.

Today we'd love you to try our orange and raisin scones, or

if you're feeling decadent our sticky toffee pudding with whiskey sauce.'

When I was finished I put the board out onto the street before coming back inside to give the place a final once over. The wooden floor was polished until it shone. The glass was gleaming, and my colourful cake stands, full of gorgeous treats, were displayed behind it. The cushions were plumped, and even the napkins were lined up perfectly. I felt like a little girl playing shop.

Dad arrived soon after. "Congratulations again on last night, Lily. I'm so proud of you. You deserve it to be a success, you've put so much into it."

We both donned our aprons, and he turned to me. "Are you ready?"

"As ready as I'll ever be," I said, nervously biting down on my lip.

"We have this under control. Let's go team McDermott!" He raised his hand in a high-five, and I slapped it back. I walked over and turned the sign from Closed to Open. Then we both took our places behind the counter and waited.

It took a while for our first customer to arrive, and for a long time it was just myself and Dad looking nervously at one another, but eventually, over two hours later, a man finally wandered through the door. He ordered a macchiato to go and a blueberry muffin. I was trembling as the coffee machine hissed and bubbled to life scenting the air with ground arabica beans. I didn't think I'd ever forget that order. I tried to act cool as I boxed up his purchase and rang it through on the till. As soon as

21

he had gone back out the door, I jumped up and down and squealed.

"I can't believe I just had a customer!" I proudly held up the ten-euro note that the man had just paid with.

Dad laughed at me. "That tends to be the idea of opening up a business, Lily! You'd better get used it to it – once word of mouth gets around, you'll have a queue out that door, I bet you."

Dad wasn't quite right. By three o'clock, we had had two more customers, but it was only day one. I knew it would take time to spread word of mouth.

* * *

"Well, I think that's what you call a success," Dad said after the last customer of the day had left and he changed the sign on the door back to Closed. I was giddy with excitement. I gave Dad a high five. "Thank you so much for today, I really appreciate you helping me out like this."

"Don't mention it, I really enjoyed myself. It felt good to have somewhere to go when I got up this morning."

My heart broke for him sometimes. I suspected that Dad was bored since he retired; he filled his days either playing golf or doing his computer course. I always felt that he was lonely, and it broke my heart that he was facing into old age without my mother by his side. Even though she had been dead since I was two years old, I knew Dad had never got over her death. He still missed her dearly; the pain of losing her had never eased for him. They should have been enjoying retirement together, perhaps seeing a bit of the world; instead, she was taken too young, leaving Dad many long years ahead as a widow and

22

struggling to raise two young daughters. He had never met anyone else, said he just wasn't interested. There would never be anybody else quite like Mam in his eyes.

"Same time again tomorrow then?" I said, grinning.

"Yes, boss!" he said cocking his hand in mock salute.

After Dad left I started work on my mixes for the following morning. I also had several batches of cupcakes to ice for the local radio stations. I was hoping they might give me a little shout out on air. I made a few extra and boxed them up to bring home to Sam.

It was after nine when I eventually climbed up on my bike to head for home. The sun was setting in glorious streaks of pink and orange. I was exhausted and yet so happy at how my first day had gone. I had loved every second of it. When I reached our apartment, I put my key in the door and went inside. I was surprised to find that Sam wasn't home yet. He had called me earlier to see how my first day was going but I hadn't had time to talk to him. I went down to our bedroom, removed my sandals, and slipped my tired feet into my comfy slippers before making my way back down to the kitchen. My first port of call before doing anything was to make myself a strong coffee from the Nespresso machine. I sat up on a chair at the breakfast bar, clasped the mug in between my hands, and looked around the kitchen. White glossy cabinets ran around the walls, and all the appliances were finished in stainless steel. It was at least three times the size of the kitchen I had left behind me in Ballyrobin. Sometimes I had to pinch myself that I actually lived here in a penthouse apartment in Dublin's city centre. I called Sam, but his phone rang out so I guessed he had to work late.

A while later the buzzer went and I thought it was Sam coming home and that he had forgotten his key, but instead I heard Frankie's voice at the other end.

"This is a nice surprise," I said, meeting her at the door. She was weighed down with newspapers and magazines. She followed me into the kitchen and let them all fall down onto the marble counter top.

"You're famous!" she said, opening up the first paper in her pile and flicking through to the social pages at the back until I saw my face grinning back at me like a loon. "You're in every paper!"

"This is great, Frankie. Thank you!"

"Don't mention it. Oh look, you've been baking," she said in mock surprise before swiping one of the cupcakes that I had brought home for Sam and taking a bite.

"You're lucky I always make extra," I said, wagging my finger at her.

"Sorry, I'm starving," she said through a mouthful.

"I can see that. Here, you've a bit of icing there." I pointed to her cheek and handed her a tissue.

Just after ten I heard the door open and Sam's footsteps coming down the hallway. He rounded the corner and came into the kitchen. "Lily, how was –" He stopped when he saw Frankie sitting there. I watched as his face fell. "Oh hi, Frankie."

I prayed she didn't notice.

"Well, you could at least try to look pleased to see me –" she said, missing nothing.

24

I cringed.

"Sorry, Frankie, I wasn't expecting you," he said feebly.

"Hmmmh, clearly not!" she replied, tossing her long hair back over her shoulder.

His brow creased down into that furrow once again, which it seemed to be doing a lot lately. Then his face clouded over, and he turned and walked back out of the kitchen.

"Who pissed on his cornflakes this morning?" Frankie asked, turning to me.

I had to stifle a giggle. "Leave him alone, he's fine," I said with a confidence that I didn't really feel. "He just has a lot on in work." But the truth was that this behaviour was totally out of character for Sam. He was never usually rude to people.

"Well, I know where I'm not wanted," Frankie said in mock affront. She stood up and started to put on her jacket.

"Frankie, please stay, he's just tired -"

"Don't worry, I have to go to a launch anyway."

"Oh, what's it for?"

"Some airline is launching a new route to Cuba – I'm only going for the cocktails. The speeches will all be over by now."

I laughed. "You have the best job."

"It has its perks!" she said with a wink before giving me a kiss on the cheek.

After Frankie had left, I went down to the bedroom where Sam was just coming out of the shower with a towel wrapped around his waist. Droplets of water glistened on the broad flank of his chest.

"So how was your first day?" he asked. "Were you busy?"

25

"Super!" I said, forcing a smile on my face. "I loved every minute of it. I didn't have many customers but it's early days. You were working late?" I asked.

"Yeah, it's manic right now," he sighed.

I walked over and put my arms around him. "Are you sure everything is okay?" I asked nervously. "It's just that you seem to be really stressed out?"

He looked at me and for a moment it looked at though he was about to tell me something but changed his mind at the last minute. "Sorry, I didn't mean to be rude. I had a day from hell." He ran his hands back through his wet hair. "I'd better go and apologise to Frankie," he said sheepishly.

"She's already left actually –"

"Oh really?" His face fell. "Because of me?"

"Well, she's heading off to some PR thing." I slipped my hand through the gap in his towel and up along the wiry hairs of his thigh. I was startled when I felt him flinch and move away from me.

"Sorry, Lily . . . I'm exhausted." He wouldn't meet my eyes and his face was wearing that same expression again.

"Oh. . ." The rejection stung. I tried not to let him see but it hurt. I turned and walked back out to the kitchen. There definitely seemed to be something up with him. It felt as though there was something that he wasn't telling me. At first I hadn't been sure whether I was being paranoid, but now I knew I wasn't just imagining it, Frankie had noticed it too. I tried to wrack my brains to think back on whether I had said or done something wrong, but I couldn't think of anything. After everything I had been through with Marc, I still found it difficult not to let my imagination run wild at times and to start thinking the worst. I had been so badly hurt before, and it had taken me a while to let my walls down to let Sam in. In the back of my mind I always had the fear that it could happen again. I didn't like this feeling; it unsettled me and made me feel insecure. I had to remind myself that Sam wasn't Marc, and if we were to have any chance of a happy relationship, then I needed to trust him, but God, it was so hard sometimes.

CHAPTER 3

I spent the next few weeks in a blur with *Baked with Love*. I would jump on my bike early every morning, cycling past the broad swell of the inky Liffey, to begin my day's baking, and then after the café closed in the evenings, I would start prepping for the following day. I was putting in fourteen-hour days, sometimes more, but I had never been happier. I dreamed in cake; divine tartlets and towers of colourful macarons seemed to fill my head constantly. I loved what I was doing. It gave me such a buzz to do simple things like twist my key in the lock to open up each morning, and I still felt a rush of excitement as I set up my displays and wrote on my chalkboard before putting it out onto the street. I loved the feeling of kneading the dough with my fingertips until it was pliable or mixing pale yellow batter until it was marshmallow soft.

Although we had a few customers, if I was honest when I had put my business plan together, I had expected more. A lot more. Sometimes hours would go by without a single person coming in the door, but Dad kept reminding me that it was still early days and it would take a while for word of mouth about *Baked with Love* to spread.

I have to say that Dad was a lifesaver; there was no way I could have done it without him. As well as giving me daily pep talks, he was doing me a huge favour by helping out every day. I wasn't earning enough yet to be able to pay him, but I think he was enjoying it. I had noticed that he seemed brighter in himself. I could tell that he enjoyed coming to work every morning and the feeling of satisfaction going home after a long, tiring day knowing he had put in a hard graft.

Sam was still going through moody periods, sometimes he was really loving but other times he was cool and distant. I had attempted to keep things breezy without continually asking him if he was okay, but the truth was that I was worried. I was trying to give him as much space as he needed, but then he would surprise me by suddenly taking me into his arms and telling me how much he loved me and that nobody had ever made him this happy. Or he would climb into bed and spoon me from behind and we would stay locked together like that all night long. But I was just so confused as to what was the matter with him and why was he blowing hot and cold?

One evening he was just coming in the door as I was putting on my jacket to leave.

"Oh, I didn't realise you were going out." His face fell.

I had called him on my way home earlier to tell him I was meeting Frankie, but he hadn't phoned me back.

"I'm just popping out to meet Frankie for a drink."

"Oh right, I wanted to talk to you about something but it can wait –"

He walked over to the fridge and took out a beer. He rooted out a bottle opener and popped the lid before raising the beer to his lips and taking a mouthful. I looked at him quizzically. It wasn't like him to drink when he had to be up for work in the morning.

"Sorry, I just really need it tonight," he said as if he could read my mind. He pinched the bridge of his nose with his thumb and forefinger and closed his eyes just for a second, but it was a fraction too long.

"Are you sure you're okay?" I asked when his eyes flickered open again.

"Of course I am, " he said, distractedly picking up his post and quickly scanning through the envelopes.

He leant in and gave me a kiss on the cheek. "Have a good night – tell Frankie I said hi."

* * *

Frankie and I made our way down to the back of the darkened wine bar located in the basement of a Georgian townhouse. Candles flickered on the tabletops, and the low vaulted brick ceilings gave the place an intimate atmosphere. We sat down in a velvet-upholstered booth and the sommelier handed us the wine list.

"So, did Sam get over his PMT?" Frankie probed after we had ordered a bottle of pinot noir. I knew she thought his behaviour the last time she was over was strange.

I smiled. "I think he was just having a bad day."

She nodded but I knew she wasn't buying it. "Hmmmh."

"Oh, Frankie, I'm at my wits' end with him," I blurted. "He's been acting strange for weeks now, he's just really . . . distant. I don't know what is going on inside his head."

"So what do you think it is?"

The waiter came over with the bottle of wine we had

31

ordered, uncorked it, and poured us both a glass.

I raised the glass to my lips and took a sip tasting notes of cranberry and liquorice. I instantly felt my shoulders begin to relax. "I don't know . . . I'm so worried that he has gone off me . . ."

"Look, you said yourself that he's under a lot of stress in work, he's probably just tired –"

Suddenly, tears filled my eyes. "It's not just recently," I said, fishing a tissue out of my handbag and using it to dab them away. God only knew what state my mascara was in. "He's been really off with me for weeks now. I think he might want to break up with me, Frankie, but he doesn't know how –"

"You don't know that! Why don't you try talking to him? Tell him how you're feeling?"

"I'm frightened. I know it's stupid, but I'm so scared that I'm going to lose him. After everything that happened with Marc I don't think I could go through that all over again."

"So what's the alternative, sit here crying your eyes out and tormenting yourself because you know something is up? You need to be straight with him, Lily. If he's messing you around, you need to know why. Hopefully, it's nothing serious and you can get things back on track between you again, but you're not doing yourself any favours by burying your head in the sand. He owes it to you to be straight up."

"I know you're right –" I exhaled heavily. Frankie was always the voice of reason.

"Talk to him tomorrow, Lily. Don't put it off any longer."

CHAPTER 4

The next morning I felt Sam stir beside me. I checked the clock and saw it was just after six. I rolled over to kiss him, but instead he turned away from me and got out of bed.

"You're going already?" I said. "I thought you wanted to talk to me about something?"

"Sorry, Lily, I've loads to get through in work, so I want to get in while the office is quiet – less distractions. Can we do it later?"

"Sure . . ." I said, lying back against the pillows.

I watched as he hurried into the bathroom, and soon the hum of the shower could be heard. He emerged a short time later in a navy suit with a crisp white shirt underneath. The collar was open, and I could see the dark hairs of his chest above it.

He leaned over the bed. "Have a good day," he said, then gave me a quick peck on the cheek and was gone.

* * *

Sunlight filtered through the old glass windows, contorting and twisting the view beyond, where inside I was carefully stacking a tower of cerise pink macarons. I was really pleased with how they had turned out; the crisp outer shell hid a lighter than air texture but the pièce de résistance was the gooey, raspberry-flavoured filling, which exploded on your tongue. I hoped the shocking colour would catch people's eyes as they went past. I looked out through the glass at the people walking up and down Bluebell Lane beyond. Some were so busy on phones or talking to their friends that they didn't even notice my café. Every so often I noticed the display would catch a person's eye, but they still kept walking. It was hard not to get disheartened by it.

I couldn't help but thinking about Sam and his eagerness to escape me earlier that morning. We really needed to talk. We couldn't keep avoiding the elephant in the room.

When I was finished in the window, I went into the kitchen where large sacks of flour and sugar leaned tiredly against one another. A lot of the ingredients were nearly at their use-by dates and I would have to throw them out, unused. I hated the thoughts of such waste, especially when the business was struggling. Had I been insane thinking I could open my own bakery? Every time I mentioned my doubts to Dad he assured me that businesses took time to get established. I knew he was right, but it was so stressful when the invoices were arriving from suppliers daily, not to mention my utility bills, and they all needed to be paid.

I set to making a sticky toffee pudding. I had made it the previous week and it had been a hit – well, if you consider that, of the seven customers I had had that day, five of them had ordered it made it a hit in my book. The benchmark of success was very low these days. It wasn't long before the air was infused with the intoxicating scent of dates, muscovado brown sugar, and spices as the dark mixture bubbled on the hob. When it was all melted, I spooned the rich treacle mixture out of the copper pot and into tins before popping them into the oven.

I went back out to the front and nearly did a happy dance

when the bell tinkled and a man I had noticed coming in the previous two days came in again and ordered a coffee to go.

"I think you have your first regular!" Dad said as soon as he had left. "You see, I told you once people come through the door and try this place they'll want to keep coming back."

I had to smile at his positivity. "Dad, I'm going to get you cheerleading pom-poms one of these days!"

After lunch a woman came through the door with a pram. Her eyes were pink-rimmed, and her hair stood in a halo of frizz around her head like it hadn't been brushed. She looked exhausted, and when I peeked into her pram, I saw the reason was a tiny bundle swaddled in pink.

"Double espresso, please," she said.

"She's gorgeous," I said, smiling.

"She is, isn't she?" the mum said. "Although she has kept me awake most of last night."

"Get that into you," I said, handing her the coffee when it was ready. "And here." I lifted a generous slice of the toffee pudding and placed it onto a plate with a heavy dollop of cream on the side. "Try this, it might give you a bit of a lift," I said with a wink.

"Thank you so much, that's very kind of you," she said. Tears began to well in the corners of her eyes, and she quickly brushed them away before they could spill down her cheeks. "Stupid hormones," she said, laughing. "But thank you – you've brightened up my day."

She took a seat on the sofa and fed her baby, and I couldn't help but notice that as she took a forkful of the pudding her body

35

seemed to relax and the corners of her lips turned upwards with a smile. It was only a small thing, but I couldn't help but feel lifted. This is what I loved most about my job. Through the magic of cake, I was able to give people a simple pleasure when they might be having a bad day. This was what made me happy.

CHAPTER 5

As I locked the door to *Baked with Love* that evening, I felt my heart start to ratchet at the thoughts of seeing Sam when I got home. I had been so busy all day that I had managed to push the worries out of my head but now I couldn't ignore it any longer. The time had come for a frank and honest conversation and I was so afraid of what I was going to uncover.

When I came in the door I was surprised to see that Sam was already sitting up at the breakfast bar. He had been working later and later over the last while, and I couldn't remember the last time he was home before me.

"Hmm, you smell delicious," he said, getting up off the stool and taking me into his arms. He kissed me on the forehead and it felt good, especially with the way he had been acting over the last few weeks. Relief flooded through me. Maybe things weren't as bad as I feared.

"Sticky toffee pudding?" he asked.

"Correct and right! Don't worry, I've brought you home a slice," I said, fishing around in my bag for the piece I had boxed up for him before I left.

"So how did it go today?" he asked.

"Well, I think I have my first regular! Although the café was still too quiet – it's a start –" His phone beeped interrupting me, and he went over and lifted it off the island.

"Hmmmh . . . that's great . . ." he said, distracted by something he was reading on it.

"What is it?" I asked.

"Sorry?" he asked, looking up at me.

"Your phone, what's so important? I was telling you about my day, Sam!"

"Oh sorry, it's an email from the New York office."

I took a deep breath. I had to say this now. I had promised myself after Marc that if I ever felt insecure or if something was bothering me in a relationship that I wouldn't be afraid to say it instead of brushing it under the carpet for the sake of avoiding an argument. I owed it to myself not to go through that again.

"Look, Sam, I know you're stressed in work but it's really affecting your mood, and I'm constantly worrying that I've said or done something wrong . . . I can't keep living like this. I feel like I don't know where I stand!"

"What do you mean, Lily?" He had the decency to look shocked at least.

"With you – with us. If your feelings have changed, then you owe it to me to be upfront, Sam."

"Lily, I'm sorry . . ." He seemed shocked. "I can promise you that my feelings haven't changed. I love you." He put his phone down on the marble worktop and made his way over to me. "I just have a lot on my mind." He placed his arms on my shoulders.

"Well, maybe you should let me in, Sam, whatever is going on with you, just tell me because I'm not stupid, I know there is something up."

He exhaled deeply. "You're right, Lily. I do owe you an explanation for my behaviour over the last few weeks."

My heart felt as though it had been replaced with a budgie fluttering around in there. "What is it, Sam?" In one way the validation of being right was good, but now that there was a problem, I was terrified.

"Maybe you should sit down . . ."

"What is it, Sam? Just spit it out!" I said once I was sitting on a chair. I felt like I had opened Pandora's box. I wasn't sure I was ready for what he was about to say.

"I'm sorry, Lily, I've been trying to find a way to tell you, but I can't seem to ever get the words out . . ."

I knew it. He wanted to break up with me. My heart crashed to the floor. My worst fears had been realised.

"I've been seconded to the New York office," he continued. "I've tried everything to get out of it, and at one point I wasn't sure if it was even going to happen, but it's looking like it's definitely going ahead now. That's why I was working crazy hours, I was hoping if I could get a load done while I'm this side of the Atlantic, they wouldn't have to send me over, but Donal confirmed it yesterday – they need me to go. I'm so sorry, I tried my best to get out of it, but they won't budge . . ."

"You're moving to New York?" I was aghast. Okay, it was a lot better than breaking up with me, but it still wasn't good news.

"Only for six months and I'll be able to get home a couple of times and you can come visit me as well –"

"You sure know how to put a positive spin on things!" I

39

said still in shock.

"Believe me, I'd rather not be going, but they've an issue on the team there so two of us have been selected to steady the ship until they appoint a new director. It's a great opportunity for my career, Lily. If I turn this down I can say goodbye to any other chance of promotion."

My legs felt as heavy as tree trunks. I was glad I was sitting down.

"Please say something, Lily, I feel terrible about all of this –"

"Well, I wish you had told me sooner. We're a couple, we should be able to talk about things like this without me imagining all sorts of other stuff going on."

"You're right, Lily. I'm sorry, in hindsight now I can see that you must have been worried, but you were so busy with *Baked with Love* and everything – this is such an exciting time for you – I didn't want to ruin it."

"So when do you go?" I asked feeling desolate.

He lowered his voice. "They want me to start in two weeks."

"Two weeks? Well, I guess it's all arranged then . . ." A few months ago I could have gone with him, I had no ties. In fact, it would have been a great adventure, but now with *Baked with Love* I wasn't going anywhere.

"I'm so sorry, Lily. I really am. I hate this just as much as you do."

"Look, Sam, I just wish you'd told me earlier instead of now when it's come as such a shock. I wasn't expecting this at all." In some ways I was relieved that things were still okay between us, but the prospect of not having him around for the next six months was awful.

"Have you a place to stay?"

"Work are organising short-term apartments."

"Well, at least I'll have free accommodation when I visit." I tried to force myself to sound cheery.

He bent down in front of me and wrapped me into his arms. "I'm going to miss you so much, you know that don't you? I really wish I didn't have to go."

"I know," I said, letting my head fall wearily against his chest. I felt so sorry for him because as much as I was going to miss him, it was Sam who had to leave everything behind him and get settled into life in a new city. I forced a smile on my face for his sake. "It's just six months, the time will fly and it'll be all over before you know it." But I wasn't sure if I was convincing Sam or myself.

CHAPTER 6

The next two weeks flew past. Even though Sam and I only had only days left together before his secondment, I was working long hours in *Baked with Love* so we didn't see nearly as much of each other as I would have liked. I had told Frankie about our big heart to heart, and she seemed relieved that that was the reason for his moodiness. She had been very upbeat when I told her the news, saying six months was nothing, but she was a person who liked her own independence. I wasn't like her; to me six months without Sam seemed interminable. I was dreading it.

The night before Sam was due to leave, he came by *Baked with Love* and as soon as I had everything ready for the following day, we went for our last meal together. He had booked us a table in Seelo's. I had always wanted to try it, but the Michelin star meant it was out of my price list. I thought it was sweet that Sam had booked it especially for us. He had ordered the tasting menu, so I knew there would be some culinary surprises and challenges ahead of me. When the waiter served the starter, I eyed up the plate wondering what exactly it was. There was some strange-looking little egg with a spongy brown lumpy stuff sitting on what looked like the world's smallest piece of toast.

"Go on, it won't kill you to try it." Sam laughed as my fussy eating habits.

I closed my eyes and lifted it up to my lips.

"Well?" Sam asked.

It tasted salty, with a slimy, bumpy texture, and I immediately spat it straight back out again onto a napkin.

"Not a fan of caviar then?" Sam asked.

"Is that what that was? Urrgh," I asked, taking a great big gulp from my water glass. All my life I had heard people raving about it, but having just tried it I couldn't figure out why. "Why on Earth would anybody pay money for that?"

When the waiter came over to top up our wine glasses, Sam put his hand over his. "I'd better not, I've to be at the airport for five."

I made a downward pout with my bottom lip. "I can't believe it's tomorrow."

"Me neither, it feels like the last supper." He sighed. "I'm really going to miss you."

I looked at his handsome face, its angles softened by the candlelight.

"The time will fly, Sam, sure we've both been so busy lately we haven't even seen that much of each other anyway."

"But at least I get to cuddle into you every night, I'll miss having you beside me in the bed."

"I know, who am I going to warm my cold feet up against now, huh?"

He laughed and reached across the table for my hand. "Is that all I mean to you? I'm going to miss you so much, Lily."

"Me too," I said and I could feel heavy tears beginning to brim in my eyes.

44

The next morning, I heard the beep of Sam's alarm pulling me out of my deep sleep. I opened my eyes. I couldn't believe the time had finally come to say our goodbyes. I got up with him, shivering in the cold morning air. I quickly belted my dressing gown around my waist.

While he was in the shower, I went into the kitchen and packaged up some of his favourite Heavenly Orange Cake that I had made especially for him the day before.

He appeared after the shower, dressed in a black V-neck cashmere sweater and jeans. He pulled me into his arms, and I could feel the softness of his freshly shaven cheek against mine. He smelt liked citrus fruit from his shower gel. I breathed in his smell once more and then he kissed me on the lips.

His phone beeped. "Taxi's outside," he said, looking down glumly at it. He took me back into his arms and squeezed me tightly. "I better go."

I nodded as he walked over and picked up his case. I walked over to the door with him.

He stopped and turned back to me. "I love you, Lily. I'll text you as soon as I land."

"I love you too." My voice threatened to break.

He wheeled his case down the hall before stopping to turn around and blow me a kiss. Then he disappeared into the lift and that was it, he was gone.

CHAPTER 7

I couldn't go back to bed after he had gone. I was too upset. Already I felt lost and lonely wandering around the empty apartment on my own and he had only been gone for a few minutes. I kept telling myself that six months was no time – it was going to fly. I knew this job was important to Sam and it could open up a lot of doors for his career but that didn't mean that I wouldn't miss him dreadfully.

When the day had broken, I decided to hop on my bike earlier than usual and head into *Baked with Love*. There were myriad things I could be doing in there to occupy myself. All I knew was that moping around, feeling sorry for myself, was not going to help me.

"Did Sam get off all right?" Dad asked when he came in later that morning. My early start meant that I was already way ahead of where I would usually be, leaving time for us to sit down with a coffee before we had to open up. Dad put a sticky bakewell slice on a plate in front of me. "Get that into you," he said.

"I can't, Dad." My stomach just wasn't able for food.

"He'll be home before you know it," he said kindly.

I nodded, not trusting myself to speak.

"And you can go visit him. You've always wanted to visit the Big Apple!"

"I don't think I can, Dad. What about this place, it's only just up and running? I can't just swan off to New York." Although I loved what I was doing, I was just starting to realise what a big commitment owning your own business actually was. Until things got properly established, there was no way I could go anywhere.

At nine o'clock we both hooked our aprons over our necks and got ready to welcome the day's customers. I was glad to be kept busy all morning in a blur of coffees to go and takeaway baked goods. We still had far too many empty tables, but it was better to have a few customers than none at all. I could make a latte or cappuccino with speed these days, tapping the portafiller expertly and frothing the milk and I was beginning to know my customers' habits; on Fridays people wanted to treat themselves, so my gooey cupcakes were popular, whereas on Mondays, healthier cakes like blueberry and banana loaf or my breakfast muffins tended to sell better.

I was just clearing up a table after a customer when I spotted the shocking pink headline on a well-thumbed copy of *Social Importance* magazine they had left behind them.

'NADIA AND MARC – CRACKS EXPOSED! A RELATIONSHIP ON THE ROCKS? SEE PAGE ELEVEN FOR FULL STORY'

I froze. I knew I shouldn't, I never felt good after reading about them, but I couldn't resist keeping track of the events of my ex-husband Marc and actress Nadia's rocky relationship. I had no contact with Marc anymore; I had severed all ties the day he had tried to ruin my relationship with Sam on what would

48

have been our first wedding anniversary. I knew he and Nadia had broken up briefly but had reunited when Nadia had given birth to a baby boy last year. According to the gossip magazines the relationship was on/off again, and now I didn't know if they were even together anymore. I knew that Marc and I would need to sit down at some point in the future and decide what we were going to do with the house we jointly owned together in Ballyrobin, but for now I was happy to block it out of my head.

It seems Marc and Nadia are at it again. The couple's famously on/off relationship seems to be taking its toll on the actress. A noticeably gaunt-looking Nadia was spotted crying on a friend's shoulder at the wrap party for her latest movie "Wreckage." The couple who met on the set of "The Recluse" and welcomed baby Marley into the world last year haven't been seen in public together since their appearance on the red carpet at the BAFTAs in London last month where Nadia was nominated for best supporting actress for her role as "Kitty Williams" in the biopic of the life of railway pioneer Charles Fury.

"Lily? Lily, are you listening to me?"

I looked around to see Dad was trying to get my attention. I quickly closed the magazine.

"Sorry, Dad, what's wrong?"

"I was just wondering if you wanted me to put another batch of scones in the oven, we're almost out?"

"Oh sorry, no, don't worry, I'll do it now. I didn't realise we were so low."

"Well, that blackberry and vanilla flavour you made seems

49

to have been a hit. You'll have to make them a regular on the menu."

I took the magazine into the kitchen with me. I didn't want Dad to see what I had been reading. I don't know why but I always felt embarrassed whenever I saw Marc and Nadia gracing magazine pages together. I think it was the reminder of my failed marriage being rubbed in my face for all and sundry to see. There was nowhere to lick my wounds in private; I had to live my humiliation in public.

I quickly mixed up a new batch of scones, feeling the therapeutic effects of kneading my hands deeply into the dough. When I had them in the oven, I opened up the magazine again. I couldn't help myself.

I looked through the paparazzi photographs of the two of them; there was one of Marc wearing a baseball cap and dark aviator sunglasses pushing Marley on a swing while he read something on his phone. There was another of Nadia carrying their son on her hip and shielding his face from the cameras as she rushed down the steps of their home and into a waiting car. You couldn't see the child's face, but he had long, curly, white-blonde hair. He looked gorgeous, but then that was to be expected with two good-looking parents.

A source close to the couple has said that Marc, who had a minor role in "The Recluse" but hasn't had any major success since, is finding it hard living in the eclipse of his partner's stellar career. Apparently, the couple has entered crisis talks assisted by renowned relationship therapist to the stars Fiona Farrington. A representative for the couple

declined to comment when asked about the story. Let's hope
they can work things out for the sake of their son, Marley.

Even though Marc had left me for this woman, I didn't feel jealous anymore. I was just sad for everyone's sake, especially for little Marley who was too young to understand the drama he was born into. Although, I had never thought I would say it, I really hoped it was working out for them. It was amazing how I had come full-circle. Sometimes I even amazed myself.

When the scones were finished I went back out to help Dad when I saw Frankie there chatting to him.

"How are you doing?" she asked, pushing her sunglasses up into her auburn hair.

"I'm okay," I said, making a sad face. "It's going to be a long six months. I'm already missing him and he hasn't even landed there yet." I sighed.

"It's only six months, Lily, that's no time. Come on," she said, putting her hand over mine."

I knew she just didn't get it. "So what can I get you?"

"I'm so hung-over. I'll have the strongest coffee you have."

"Where were you last night?" I asked, grinding beans to make her a double espresso.

"At a launch party for 'Second Skin.' So how about we head out for some cocktails tonight to cheer you up – I hate seeing my best friend so sad."

"I thought you were hung-over?" I said.

"I am but I'll need a cure later, won't I? I'll call back after eight, will you be ready then?"

"I guess . . ." I wasn't in the mood of going out socializing, but I knew that heading back to a lonely apartment all by myself would only make me feel worse. I needed to keep myself as distracted as possible or else the next six months would feel like an eternity.

"Great, see you later!"

I had just finishing icing a carrot cake with orange-flavoured frosting when I checked my phone and saw I had a text from Sam:

"Just landed now and on my way to the apartment. Missing you so much already xxx"

I felt tears spring into my eyes. My heart physically ached for him. How was I going to survive for the next six months?

CHAPTER 8

Somehow I made it through the next few days. Sam and I kept in touch mainly with Skype. The time difference was a pain; it meant he usually called me when I was mid-chaos in *Baked with Love*. I would run into the kitchen for a minute to chat to him, but inevitably Dad would need to ask me something or else after having had no customers for hours, several would arrive at once and I would see Dad struggling to keep on top of the queue. Or when I finally got home in the evenings and was free to talk, Sam was already busy in the office. Other times the screen would freeze or there was a time delay as we spoke, so it was very difficult to have a proper chat. He seemed to really like his new role though, and although the work was challenging, he was getting great experience.

Baked with Love was still struggling. Some days it was so bad that I could count on one hand the number of customers that we had. I would lie awake for hours at night worrying about it. I was so afraid this business was going to fail. Whenever I mentioned it to Dad, he would shrug me off telling me it was still early days, but the truth was I was really starting to panic. Every night I was dropping off tray-loads of unsold goods into the nearby homeless shelter. Father Joe who ran the centre gladly accepted whatever I had left over, he said sometimes a mug of warm tea and a sticky cinnamon bun were the only good things that these people had in their day, and I was glad that I could help them out in my own small way rather than seeing it all go to waste.

I had told Frankie about my concerns the night we had gone out together.

"I think I've bitten off more than I can chew," I had sighed.

"There's no point in having the world's loveliest bakery – and it is the world's loveliest bakery – if nobody knows you exist! You need to up the marketing. Why don't you drop in free tea or coffee vouchers to the offices nearby?" she had said.

"But I can't afford to give away stuff for free! I'm trying to save my business not send the whole thing further under!" I argued back with her.

"No, of course not, but you take the risk that they'll buy something when they're in there, and if not, then at least they know where the place is and you hope they'll be future customers."

"It's worth a try, I guess," I said uncertainly. At this stage I was so desperate that I would do anything, so the next day I had called up the company who printed my business cards and asked them to design some fliers for me. I really hoped it would work and wouldn't be the final nail on the coffin for *Baked with Love*.

* * *

I was working away in the café one day when the bell sounded with its little trrring and I saw the woman with the baby come through the door. I had got to know her name over the last few weeks as Claire and her baby was Ellie.

I smiled as she came up to the counter. "She's getting big,"

I said, gesturing to the pram. Even in the space of a few weeks, I could see that she had grown a lot.

"This place is my saviour," she said, eyeing up the cakes. "It's five minutes of heaven in the day."

So, are you getting any more sleep?" I asked.

"No," she sighed. "I think I've accepted that she might sleep by the time she's eighteen and anything before that is a bonus."

"That's a good outlook," I laughed.

I made her usual latte and then placed a steaming brownie on a plate for her. She needed something warm and chocolatey to give her a lift.

"How did you know I was going to choose that?" she said, looking at me open-mouthed.

"Oh, you pick up a thing or two when you do my job; you get to know what people need."

Claire pushed the pram over and sat down on the sofa. She lifted Ellie up, and I watched as her eyes, two huge pools of blue, popped open and looked around until she focused on her mother. Then her little face broke into a gummy smile, and I watched as Claire beamed back at her. I felt my heart soar watching the two of them caught up in their own little bubble.

My phone rang lifting me out of my thoughts. I saw it was Clara and was torn between ignoring it, but then guilt got me at the last minute and I pressed the answer button.

"Hi, Clara," I said. "What's up?"

"You haven't seen the boys in weeks, they'll have forgotten what you look like -" She got straight to the point as usual.

"Sorry, Clara, I've been so busy lately between *Baked with Love* and Sam leaving . . ."

"We're all busy, Lily, but you have to make time for people. Call over on Saturday."

"Right," I sighed. "I'll see you then."

I knew her motivations had nothing to do with the boys and instead was a veil for her to interrogate me. She liked to find out what areas of my life were weak, and then she would attack me right there in that very spot.

"What is it?" Dad asked after I had hung up.

"I've been summoned. Clara has invited me over on Saturday."

He laughed.

"Please come with me, Dad, don't make me go on my own!" Dad would always step in when she went too far.

"I can't, Lily, sorry, I've a golf tournament."

"I guess I'm going solo then," I said, groaning.

* * *

The following Saturday I followed Clara down along the chequered tiles into the kitchen where her husband, Tom, was reading the newspaper at one end of the table while the boys were playing with Play-Doh at the other.

"Good to see you, Lily," Tom said, folding down the broadsheet and leaving it on the table in front of him.

"What are you making?" I asked Jacob, taking a seat beside him.

"The seven wonders of the world."

"I see . . ." These kids are prodigies – I couldn't even name the seven wonders of the world let alone make them.

Clara busied herself making some tea that she insisted I had to try for its purifying properties. It probably came from the ground-down toenail fungus of some virgin girl living in the Amazon rainforest.

"For God's sake, Lily – don't let them mix up the colours!" Clara said, grabbing a piece of green Play-Doh and a blue piece out of Joshua's hands before setting the teapot down on the table and joining us.

Tom risked a wry smile from the side of his mouth.

"So how's business?" Tom asked.

"To be honest it's slow, some days are better than others, but I'll be honest, it's taking longer than I thought to get up and running."

"That's always going to be the way it is with a new business. It takes time to get word of mouth out there," Tom said encouragingly.

"What you need to do is to cut costs – improve your margins!" Clara interjected. "Instead of butter, use margarine. Instead of those fancy napkins, go for the two-ply ones, they will suffice just as well."

"But I like those napkins!" I said. I knew I was a touch defensive, but hearing criticism from Clara was like someone criticizing my child. I had built that business from nothing, starting in my tiny kitchen back in Ballyrobin. I had poured blood, sweat, and tears into it. I liked that I didn't skimp on the little details. When other bakeries were using artificial butter, I insisted on using the real deal because I knew it was what made my cakes golden and spongy. It was those little things that I hoped would set *Baked with Love* apart from all the other bakeries around town. I didn't want to cut corners, but sometimes I felt so disheartened. I was putting everything into it but nothing seemed to be working.

"Okay, well, if your business goes down the toilet you can cry into your fancy napkins," Clara said.

"Now, Clara," Tom said kindly, "I think Lily knows what she's doing."

"I really appreciate everything you've done for me, Tom," I said. "There would be no bakery if it wasn't for you."

"Don't mention it – think of it as payback for all the times you've helped us out minding the kids."

"They're her nephews! It's a privilege for her to spend time with them," Clara stated.

"So how's Sam getting on the secondment?" Tom asked, changing the subject.

"Great, he seems to be really enjoying himself. I miss him though."

"It's only for six months. Pull yourself together and stop moping," Clara said.

"I'm not moping."

"Honestly, you snowflakes . . ." She shook her head pityingly at me.

"Clara, you're only three years older than me!"

"Exactly," she said, nodding self-satisfactorily.

I groaned. I would never win with Clara, so I don't know why I bothered.

CHAPTER 9

Rain trickled down the windows in fast-flowing rivulets. Outside people held umbrellas high above their heads and dodged puddles below their feet. My heart sank; I knew this weather would be bad business. Nobody in their right mind would venture out on a day like this. Dad hurried through the door a short while later and shook the droplets off his umbrella. The ends of his trousers were soaking where the rain had seeped up through the fabric.

"The Irish weather is really playing a blinder," I muttered.

"It's only a shower, the sun will be out before you know it."

"Dad, it's torrential rain out there!" I had to laugh at his optimism. He always looked for the brighter side of every situation, but I had to say he was an antidote to my darker mood over the last while. "You go and dry off those trousers, and I'll make us a cuppa."

For the first two hours after we had opened, nobody came through the door. Not a single person. The streets were empty as the rain continued to fall steadily. I looked at all my baked goods with dismay. I knew I was going to be giving most, if not all, of it to the homeless shelter again that night.

I heard the bell ring, and I startled to see an older lady rush in through the door holding a little girl by the hand. She shook off her umbrella.

I smiled a warm hello. "It's miserable out there," I said sympathetically as she took off the child's raincoat.

"We're supposed to be going to Lottie's music class, but we're after getting soaked. Then I saw this place, like a haven, and I've never been so glad to see somewhere to shelter."

She walked up to the counter.

"Come on, Lottie, let's treat ourselves after that ordeal." The little girl smiled up at her while she looked at the display with confusion. "I don't know what to give you, Lottie love," she eventually said, looking down at her granddaughter.

"Chocolate cake, Nana," Lottie said, nodding her head with certainty. "I like chocolate cake."

The woman laughed. "Oh, I know you do, sweetheart, but I don't think your mum and dad would be too happy with me if I gave you that –"

"How about a honey cookie?" I said. "I've substituted the sugar with honey so they're a bit healthier for little people."

"Me want honey cookie," Lottie said, jumping up and down.

"Oh, thank God," the woman said, sighing with relief. "My son and daughter-in-law are very keen on healthy eating. It's all sugar-free this and dairy-free that . . . and don't talk to me about e-numbers . . . They have so many rules that I get confused about what Lottie can and cannot have to be honest. My head is addled! I'll take one of those and put another in a bag for later. Bribery," she said with a wink.

"Absolutely! Anyway, it's a grandmother's prerogative to

spoil her grandkids, isn't it?"

She beamed at me like finally somebody understood her. "Yes, it is," she said conspiratorially, "but don't tell that to my son!"

We both laughed. "And what can I get for you?"

"I'll have a pot of tea and . . ." She glanced longingly at the cakes behind the glass. "I know I shouldn't really . . . but that lemon curd cake looks so good . . ."

"Good choice," Dad said over my shoulder before she could change her mind. "It's delicious."

"You sit down there and get settled, and we'll bring your tea and cake right over," I said.

They walked down and took a seat in the nook. Lottie and her grandmother were our only customers for the rest of the morning. Sometimes she would catch my eye and give me a sympathetic smile, which just made me feel worse about how quiet we were.

After a while, when the rain had petered out to a drizzle, they packed up their stuff to leave. She stopped and came over to me on her way out the door.

"I just wanted to tell you that I haven't tasted a curd like that since I was a child. It was delicious, the way it melted on the tongue and then the buttery shortcrust!" She smacked her lips together. "I'll be dreaming of it for the rest of the day!"

"Lily likes to use the old-fashioned recipes," Dad said, talking for me.

"Well, you can taste the difference, I'd forgotten what real cake tastes like! All these places are too busy cutting out things

63

and adding in other stuff so they can make them cheaper, but they don't taste like they used to. Well done you for bucking the trend! This is such a gem of a place you have here, so many of those chain places are taking over this street. Did you see there's a new Starbucks opening up around the corner?" she said shaking her head.

"Really?" My heart sank. "I didn't know that."

"They're fitting it out at the moment. It'll be open in a few weeks," she continued.

This was news to me. How was I ever meant to compete with that? It was hard enough getting customers in the door without this too!

"It's lovely to have somewhere homely to come to with Lottie when her parents are at work. I'm going to tell all my friends about this place," she continued.

"Thank you," I said. It was lovely to get good feedback, but it just seemed so slow to catch on that I was really starting to question myself for opening a business at all. And now if Starbucks were coming too, maybe I should just lock the door and give up altogether!

Later that evening after I had said goodbye to Dad, I went into the kitchen and started prepping for the next day. I looked in dismay at the trays of cakes and buns that I was going to be dropping off at the shelter on my way home. There were way more than usual owing to the bad weather. At least Father Joe would be happy, I thought.

As I mixed up my batter and watched the golden butter swirl and melt in through the flour until it became a lovely buttercup yellow, I thought about what Clara had said to me about cutting my costs. But I couldn't bring myself to do it. Maybe I was a fool, but when customers like the lady earlier commented on the taste of my cakes, it made me feel I was making a difference in their lives. Okay, I knew I was hardly saving the world but in my own small way I was putting a smile on my customers' faces and that made me happy. I loved seeing people come in to relax for half an hour enjoying a little treat and some time to themselves, and I took pride that I could do that for them. I felt I was bringing a small bit of joy to people in their busy lives. A slice of cake could be like a hug on a bad day. I of all people knew that cake had healing powers. Cake had literally transformed my life, I had managed to make what was a hobby into a career, and a tower of fallen cupcakes had led me to Sam. I was fully convinced of the magic it could bring to someone's life, and I wanted to be able to do that for other people.

I buried my hands into the dough. I kneaded it and plied it, letting all the stress out through my fingertips. I got caught up in my work, letting myself unwind from the tension of the day. I was definitely happiest in my kitchen; I wished I could lock myself in there and away from the world and the worries that came with running a business.

I heard my phone go on the worktop beside me and quickly removed my gloves and scrambled to get it. I saw it was Sam calling me on Skype. I pressed the answer button and his image appeared on the screen. I could see the outline of skyscrapers through the glass in the background.

"You're still in work? I thought you'd be finished by now?" he asked. It was almost eight p.m.

"Still here," I sighed. "I've so much to do. I'll be here for another hour anyway."

"So how was your day?" he asked me.

"Great! Everything is going great." I forced myself to sound cheery. "What about you, how's it all going?"

"We're getting on well, Ja–" The screen froze as it buffered.

"Sorry, what?" I asked when it had finally stopped and he appeared in front of me again.

"Jane, she's great. She's really easy to work with so we're getting through the work quickly."

"Oh, that's good," I said. "It's nice to have someone who gets what it's like." Jane was the other person that had been seconded from Sam's office. The two of them were steering the project together.

"Yeah, this city is great. They really know how to party!"

"Sounds like fun," I said and even I could hear the sulky tinge to my voice. I knew I was being irrational, but I was tired and cranky. It seemed that he and Jane were living it up and having the time of their lives together, without a care in the world, meanwhile I had never been so stressed.

"Look, I'd better go. I need to get decorating these buns or I'll be here all night," I said after we had chatted a bit longer.

When I finally got home that evening I collapsed in a heap on the sofa. I was exhausted. My feet were throbbing from running around all day, and my head was pounding with stress. I was hungry, but I was too tired to move to get something to eat. It was difficult to get used being alone every night. I missed Sam so much; it was so hard to go from seeing him every day to virtual chats on Skype. I hated the distance between us. I just wanted the six months to be over and then things could go back to the way they were before.

I reached for my laptop and opened up Facebook. As I scrolled down through my newsfeed, I saw photos shared from everybody else's happy lives and it just made me feel even more miserable. Suddenly I saw Sam was tagged in a photo. I clicked onto it and it looked like he was in a bar with some work colleagues. I noticed that Jane was tagged too. I knew I was being nosy but I couldn't help myself and clicked onto her profile. I had never met her before so I was curious to see what she looked like but I wished I hadn't when I saw how pretty she was. In the photo she was standing on the deck of a yacht with her arm swung around another girl, and her dark hair was blowing behind her in the wind. She was wearing a white kaftan, and her long limbs were golden and sun-kissed. Her head was thrown back in laughter showing perfect, pearly white teeth. She really was stunning. I couldn't believe she and Sam were spending all that time on their own together. In another country. I felt my stomach lurch as a little tremble of fear washed over me. I knew I had to trust him but how was I supposed to do that when he was spending all his time with Giselle bloody Bundchen?

CHAPTER 10

It was a glorious morning as I cycled down Bluebell Lane the next day. Although it was chilly, I was relieved to see that the sky was brilliant blue and there wasn't a cloud in sight. It was as if all the rain of the previous day had washed the sky clean. Seagulls caterwauled above the Dublin chimney tops and the low autumn sunlight glinted off the glass of the surrounding office blocks. The leaves on the trees around me had turned fabulous shades of burnt orange, saffron, and ochre.

I hadn't slept well thinking about Sam and Jane. My mind had been racing imagining all kinds of awful scenarios but the sunshine on my cheeks was a welcome lift, helping to shake off my tired fog. Mounting my bike every morning and sailing through the city streets was one of my favourite parts of my day. No matter what was going on inside my head or how many worries I had, I always felt better afterwards.

As I got to work that morning, I set my chalkboard out on the cobblestones, followed by the tables and chairs. We were still far too quiet so I hoped the chance to sit in the sunshine might lure in some more customers. I had dropped off the fliers for free tea/coffee into some of the nearby office blocks like Frankie had suggested, and so far I had had a good few people in to redeem them. They usually purchased a little treat too, so it had worked, but my customer numbers were still nowhere near what I needed to keep the business going. And I was only paying a token rent, what would happen when Tom wanted me to pay the proper market value? There was no way I could afford to with the customer numbers we had now.

When I was finished I stood on the street for a moment and let myself soak up the sunshine. I couldn't help smiling at my bakery. I knew I was biased but it really was the nicest shop on the street. I never got sick of looking at it. Despite my worries, I couldn't help but feel lifted on a day like this. Sam flitted into my head and I wondered what he was doing right now. I hoped he was safely tucked up in bed and wasn't still out partying with Jane.

I went back inside to get ready for the day ahead. Dad arrived a short while later and started to get the front of house ready while I concentrated on the baking in the kitchen. It was amazing how we had each slotted into our roles and knew automatically what needed to be done before the doors opened every morning. We were a good team. I began stacking some cupcakes inside the window and looked out at the busy street that was coming to life beyond. The streets were teeming with people but yet so few seemed to be stepping through the door. It was so disheartening. I was tempted to run out onto the street and physically shove them into my café so they could see for themselves what a wonderful place *Baked with Love* was. I really believed in my bakery, I just needed everyone else to too.

* * *

Later that evening, long after Dad had gone home, I sat in the kitchen and skimmed a spoon across a bowlful of lavender cream. I lifted a hefty spoonful up towards my lips. The subtle floral taste exploded on my tongue – it was just the right amount, delicate without being overpowering. "Mmmmh," I said out loud to myself. It was divine. "Just perfect!" I could happily sit there and eat the whole bowl of it by myself except I needed it to serve with the Earl Grey cake that I had just mixed. I allowed myself one more spoonful before I put the bowl into the fridge. I reckoned I deserved a little bit of a treat after the day I had had. A child had pulled a mug of coffee down off the table and spilled it all over himself. Thankfully the coffee had cooled down and he was all right, but it had given me such a fright. Then the postman arrived with a wad of bills, one of which was my rates bill. I had had to read it twice to make sure that the figure was correct. I had no idea how I was going to find the money to pay it. And this was all before the new Starbucks had even opened. They were hanging the sign the last time I had passed by so I knew it would be open any day now. Owning my own business was way more taxing than I could ever have imagined. I was stressed and exhausted all the time worrying about cash flow and supplier terms and trying to get customers through the door. It was at times like this that I felt an acute wave of longing for Sam. I missed him so much; it felt almost physical. I longed for his reassuring arms around me, telling me that everything was going to be okay. I checked the clock and calculated the time difference for when he would be leaving the office and I could call him. I just wanted to hear his comforting tones at the other end.

As soon as it hit five p.m. his time, I picked up my phone

and dialled his number.

"Lily! How are you?" he answered. There was a lot of noise in the background. My heart sank when I realized he was obviously in a bar. Again.

"Great, everything is great!" I didn't want to spoil my few minutes with him by boring him with the details of my awful day. "So where are you?" I asked.

"Oh, myself and Jane decided to head out after work and sample some of the New York night life. You should see this place – it's a restaurant but there are even beds in it! It's insane!"

The mention of her name made me bristle. I knew he was working long days so it was only natural that he was spending a lot of time with her, but he had been dropping her name into all our conversations lately and I couldn't help feeling a little bit irritated.

"Sounds cool. I miss you." I said forcing myself to sound cheery.

"Sorry, I couldn't hear you there?"

"I said I miss y–"

Just then a screech of laughter cut through the air.

"Oh my god, you won't believe it but there's actually a fire-eater walking around here now!" Sam said.

"Great," I said. I was trying so hard to keep the annoyance from my voice, but every time we spoke, he seemed to be having the time of his life. It didn't sound like he even missed me. "Look, I'd better go and let you get back to your night."

"Okay, no worries, I'll call you tomorrow, Lily."

72

"Sam, I love –"

But he had hung up the phone before I had even finished the sentence. I felt desolate. I couldn't stop thinking about him and Jane and all the fun they were having together in New York. I felt consumed with jealousy. I knew I was being petulant and I had absolutely no reason not to trust him, but I felt that sickly feeling of my old insecurities raising their head again. Because Sam and Jane were the only two seconded from their office, they were naturally going to be spending all their time together but jeez, he didn't need to make it sound like they were having so much fun! I knew I needed to trust Sam, but it was so hard after everything that had happened with Marc.

CHAPTER 11

A few days later I twisted my key in the lock and pushed the door open. As usual my ear waited for the sweet ring of the bell. I walked over the wooden floorboards and went through to the kitchen. I fired up the ovens and set to work making my scones. I mixed the flour and butter together with my key ingredient, a tiny splash of soda water, which always made my scones light and fluffy. I was just brushing their tops with egg wash before I would put them in the oven when I heard the bell tinkle outside.

"You open?" I heard Frankie's voice call to me.

"I'm in here," I shouted out to her.

"What has you up so early?" I asked, wiping my hands on my apron when she appeared in the kitchen doorway. She was wearing a black leather biker jacket over a very short dress. I took in her unruly hair and smudged eye make-up and wondered if she was trying out a new look. Nothing would surprise me with her job as a stylist. "Where are you off to?"

"It's not early – it's late. I haven't been to bed yet."

"Are you drunk?" I asked, realizing her speech was slurred.

"Noooo."

"You are!"

"I may have had a couple." Her eyes were wild and glassy.

"Well, it looks like you've had a lot more than a couple!"

"Why don't you turn that little sign of yours back around to

Closed and you and me go have some fun?"

"Frankie, it's eight a.m. in the morning!"

"So?"

"The only thing I will be drinking at this time of the day is coffee."

"Pleeeeease." She clasped her hands together as if she was praying. "Come on, Lily, it'll be like old times again."

"I have a business to run!"

"You're no fun anymore. You're always working," she said sulkily.

"I'm sorry, Frankie, but I just can't shut up shop and head off on a bender with you! Anyway, don't you have work to go to yourself?"

"I called in sick."

"Frankie! That doesn't look good."

"Jesus, chill the boots, Lily! When did you get all sensible? I think I preferred you when your life was falling apart . . ."

"Good morning," Dad said, coming through the kitchen door. "Oh hi, Frankie."

"Hi, Mr Mc! Right, I'll head on then seeing as you're zero craic."

Dad did a double-take as Frankie marched out past him. "What was that about?" he asked after she had gone.

"I'm not sure," I said. I felt uneasy. I had been so caught up with *Baked with Love* and then with Sam moving to New York that I wasn't as tuned into Frankie as I normally would be. She seemed to be going out all the time lately. Whenever I talked to her she was either on her way to or from a launch for some new product. She was forever flitting between parties, downing free cocktails and champagne. I always thought that lifestyle was part and parcel of her job. She was young, free and single so of course she wanted to have fun but there was a niggle in the back of my head that made me worry.

The door opened suddenly pulling me out of my thoughts. I saw Lottie and her grandmother coming in again. And true to her word she had brought two more people with her too. I almost ran out from behind the counter to hug her with gratitude.

"Good to see you again," Dad said greeting her. "Hi Lottie!"

"I haven't stopping raving to Hilda and Rose about this place since the last time I was here so I think it's time I brought them so they could finally see for themselves and get me to shut up!" She laughed.

"That's very kind of you," I said.

"Since I'm almost a regular I think it's time we learnt each other's names, don't you? Mabel Fox," she said, offering her hand to me first and then Dad.

"I'm Lily," I said.

"And I'm Hugh – I'm Lily's Dad," he said, shaking her hand.

"You must be very proud of your daughter, she is very talented – a born baker! It's good of you to give her a hand."

Dad shrugged his shoulders. "That's what family are for!"

"It is indeed." Mabel smiled widely at him. She had such a warm smile; it stretched from her mouth right up to the creases at the corners of her eyes. Her lined face showed a lot of laughter.

Her friends' chose their cakes and Lottie insisted on her usual honey cookie before sitting down while Mabel paid.

"I'll give you a hand down with the tray, you go and sit down," I said to Mabel when I had everything loaded onto it.

"No, I'll do it," Dad said taking it from me and rushing out from behind the counter.

I watched as he walked towards the table with Mabel. He eased her tray down onto the table and as he stood talking with her for a moment, I noticed he had started to blush.

* * *

After lunch I went into the kitchen and opened up my laptop. Sam and I had arranged to Skype just before he would be heading into the office. I dialled his number but it didn't connect. I guessed he was probably on the subway or something, but when the rest of the day went past and I didn't hear from him, I started to get worried. I hated the distance between us; it was so hard sometimes. The logical part of my brain told me to relax, that he was probably just tied up working late on something. I knew he was under a lot of pressure and he really wanted to prove himself. I made myself a cup of tea and calmed myself down, then I sent him a text saying I loved him and missed him.

When he still hadn't called me back when I was finally climbing into bed that night. I started to panic. What if something had happened to him over there? How would I know? Would his co-workers know to call me if there was an emergency? I began to catastrophise and imagined all kinds of horrible scenarios, each one worse than the last. I decided to log into Facebook to see when he had been last active. Within seconds I saw Jane had tagged him in a photo in a nightclub. There they were with cocktails in their hands and big cheesy grins. They had a feather boa wrapped around both their necks. Her blonde balayage framed a pretty sun-kissed face showing off her perfect smile. It was a kick to the stomach. He was out with her again, yet he couldn't manage to fit a five-minute conversation with me into his day? My heart sank. I shut down the laptop; I didn't want to look at it anymore. What was happening to us? There was an ocean between us but tonight it felt like so much more. Did he even want to be with me anymore? I knew a long-distance relationship required work, but it didn't seem like Sam was putting in any effort. He was too busy out partying with Jane. I felt the weight of tears building behind my eyes. How could he be so thoughtless? He knew everything that had happened between Marc and I, so he knew how hard it had been for me to let my guard down and to trust him, and this was how he treated me?

I didn't sleep that night. I tossed and turned worrying about what Sam was up to. I listened as the birds started their morning chorus and bin lorries roared down the street. So when my phone rang just after six a.m., I reached for it straight away and felt a mix of relief and anger when I saw it was Sam.

* * *

"Lily, I'm so sorry. I totally forgot to call you back –" His voice was panicked and sounded rough like gravel.

I sat up straight against the pillows. "Working late were

79

you?"

"We all went for dinner, then we went to this club, and I don't know . . . I lost track of time. I'm sorry, I don't know what to say . . ."

"Who were you out with?" I took a deep breath while I braced myself for the answer that I knew was coming.

He paused. "Jane and few of the others from the office."

"You seem to be out with her a lot –"

"Well, we were seconded together . . . there were others there too, Lily."

"Seconded to work – not to party!"

"Lily, we're working really hard over here, so I don't see what's wrong about going out for a few drinks at the end of a long day?"

"But it's every day!"

"I'm sorry – I just forgot!"

"I wouldn't forget to call you because I think about you all the time! You know what? I don't think your heart is even in this anymore –"

"Lily – I missed one phone call. Stop overreacting!"

"It's not just one phone call; every time I call you, it's all Jane this and Jane that!"

"What are you talking about, Lily? Jane is my colleague!"

"Well, do you know what, Sam? I've heard that before and it ended in divorce!"

"Lily, I think you're being completely unfair here. I'm not Marc!"

"Well, stop acting like it then!"

"What has got into you?" He exhaled heavily like he was losing patience, which only served to increase my anger. "Look, I'm sorry I forgot to call you, it was a genuine mistake, but I'm going to go now. I'm not listening to any more of this shit. Give me a call when you calm down." And then he hung up on me.

I flopped back against the headboard. My hands were trembling. I was fuming. How dare he! He had dismissed me like I was an annoying child who was imagining things and then cut me off. He was in the wrong and he was too stubborn to admit it. Well, I certainly was not going to let a man make a fool of me again. Sam Waters could go to hell.

CHAPTER 12

As I cycled to work the following morning I felt as though rage was pushing the pedals of the bike for me. Normally I took my time over the old city cobbles, but today I powered over them so that my bum bumped along on the saddle.

After I had locked it on the railings on Bluebell Lane, I stormed through the door and headed straight into the kitchen. I pounded ingredients together, slammed doors, and blustered around the place getting ready for the day ahead. My cakes were certainly not *Baked with Love* that morning.

"Is everything okay?" Dad asked a while later after I had placed my mug of tea down so hard on the counter that a bit sloshed over the side.

"Yes, of course, why?" I asked, forcing a smile on my face. I didn't want to worry him by revealing what had happened with Sam.

"You just seem a bit . . . on edge today?"

"Do I? Sorry, I'm just tired. I didn't sleep well last night."

"Go in the back there and put your head down for five minutes while it's quiet."

I looked around at the wilderness that was my bakery. "Quiet is one way of describing it!" I said grumpily.

I made myself a cup of tea. Then I did as I was told and went into the kitchen. I sat down at the bench and exhaled heavily. I picked up my phone to see if Sam had called me back but there was nothing from him, which just incensed me even further. Shouldn't he be bombarding me with apologies? I decided to dial Frankie's number.

"Uhhhh."

"Frankie?"

She groaned. "Why are you calling me so early?"

"Well, it's not that early, I thought you'd be in work already?"

"My head is banging . . . I'm so hung-over."

"Again?" I knew I sounded preachy but it seemed as though every time I spoke to her nowadays she was hung-over.

"Lily, I'm a single woman in my thirties. I'm allowed to have a bit of fun."

"Okay, calm down, there's no need to be so defensive . . . Sam and I had a huge row earlier –"

"What happened?"

"It's this Jane woman; he's always out with her. He was meant to call me last night and he totally forgot!"

"Lily, it's one phone call, chill the boots!"

"But that's the thing, it's not just one phone call. It's more than that, don't you see what it represents?"

"Yeah, that he forgot to call you . . ."

"I would never forget to call him – I think about him all the time. He's having so much fun over there that he's starting to forget about me."

"I think you're overreacting."

"That's what he said –" I said, feeling the wind being taken

84

out of my sails. I suddenly was feeling less sure of myself.

"Okay, he should have called you but Sam loves you, you need to calm down and look at the bigger picture here. You have to give him the benefit of the doubt. If he says nothing untoward happened and you love him, then you have to trust him."

"But what if he makes a fool of me?" I whispered. "I could never go through all of that again." When I thought back to the pain I had felt after Marc's betrayal and how long it had taken me to get over that hurt, I had come so far, I couldn't let myself go back to that place ever again.

"I know you've been hurt before, but you can't not trust someone because of what Marc did to you. You owe it to Sam to be fair. How can you expect your relationship to survive if you don't trust him? That isn't fair to anyone. And for what it's worth, I think Sam is one of the good ones. I really don't think he'd do that to you."

"Do you think?"

"Look, why don't you call him back and explain that you had a bad day. Sam loves you, he'll understand. Stop letting Marc ruin your chance to be happy."

I knew she was right; I would forever hate Marc for stripping away my naturally trusting nature. He had eroded my confidence, but if I let him ruin my relationships, he would always have a hold over me and I would never get to experience happiness.

I sighed. "Urggh, I hate this distance between us; it's turning me into a crazy lady."

"You were a crazy lady long before Sam moved to New

York. Now call him, I'm going back to sleep!"

After I had hung up from Frankie, I dialled Sam's number. It would be six a.m. in New York so at least I knew he would be getting up for work around then and for once wouldn't be in some bar or nightclub.

"Lily?" I heard his voice in that gorgeous husky tone that told me he had just woken up. I could imagine him in his boxer shorts, with his eyes half-open, his hair tousled from sleep. I loved when it sounded like this in the mornings, usually he would take me into his arms and I would lay my head against the dark skin of his chest.

"I'm sorry –" I blurted. "I totally overreacted last night. I just find it difficult, you know? I mean, I knew it was going to be difficult, but I didn't think it would be this hard. I didn't mean to go off at you like that –"

"Hey look, it's okay." His voice was soothing. "I get that this is hard for you – hell, it's hard for me too. And I'm sorry I forgot to call you. I promise I won't let it happen again."

"I miss you so much, Sam. I can't wait until this secondment is over and I get to have you back to myself again."

"Me too, Lily, you have no idea how much."

"Sam?" a voice called in the background. It was a female voice. My blood ran cold. "Sam?" the voice called again.

"Who is that?" I asked quickly. My heart was racing as I waited for him to answer.

"Okay, please don't overreact – it's Jane – but it's not what you think – I swear to you, Lily –" I could hear the panic in his tone. He knew he had crossed the line. Why would she be in his apartment first thing in the morning unless something had happened the night before? As the realization took hold that I wasn't just imagining things, I was left reeling. I had heard these words before from Marc; I couldn't believe that now Sam was saying the same thing to me. I heard the blood rush into my ears and I dropped the phone from my trembling hands. It fell on the floor tiles by my feet.

"Lily? Lily, are you there?" I could hear him call.

I didn't want to talk to him; I didn't want to hear him spill out any more lies to me. How had I let this happen to me again? Had I learnt nothing from Marc?

Tears started spilling down my face. I had opened the door to my heart to let Sam in, it had taken me a long time to be able to trust somebody again after what Marc had done to me, but I had believed Sam was worth it. I had taken a chance on him even when everything inside of me screamed not to do it. I should have listened though because once again I had been made a fool of.

CHAPTER 13

I sat trembling in the kitchen. The oven was bleeping, but I couldn't move myself from the chair to get up and turn it off. The thought of Sam and Jane together was like acid slowly stripping away my skin. How could he do that to me? Did he think now because there was an ocean between us that the rules had shifted and blurred somehow? He was lucky there was an ocean between us because if I saw him right now, who knows what I might do to him!

"Aren't you going to turn that off?" Dad said, coming into the kitchen and heading straight over to the oven. His eyes landed on me then. "Are you okay, Lily? You're looking very pale?"

I brushed a piece of hair back from my face and forced a smile. "I'm great, Dad."

"You would tell me if something was worrying you, wouldn't you?" he said looking at me with his head cocked to the side.

"Of course!" I tried to sound breezy, but I wasn't sure I quite pulled it off.

"Everything is okay with the business, isn't it?"

"It's all good, Dad. What's with all the questions?"

"I'm your father, that's what I'm supposed to do!"

I went to stand up but suddenly I felt lightheaded. My

whole body felt heavy. "Actually, Dad, I'm not feeling so good." I sat back down again onto the bench. "I think I might need to go home and lie down. Will you be okay on your own?" I craned my neck to look beyond the kitchen door and took a swift glance around the place. There was one customer, a man working on his laptop. He had it plugged in to the wall, and suddenly I felt angry that the electricity he was using would negate the profit I would earn from his cup of tea. Then I chastised myself for being so mean. One customer using my electricity was better than none at all. I wanted everyone to feel welcome in *Baked with Love* no matter how much they spent.

Dad looked at me with concern. This was totally out of character for me and he knew it. "Of course, I can hold the fort here. You go home and go straight to bed, do you hear me?"

For once I wasn't going to argue, and I got up again and steadied myself. I lifted my coat down from the stand and slid my arms into its sleeves. I would come in extra early in the morning to catch up on what I'd usually do in the evening.

Once outside the fresh air was a welcome relief. I breathed it deeply into my lungs. In, out, in, out, until I began to feel less wobbly. When my legs felt strong enough I got up on my bike and headed back home. Horrible thoughts of Sam and Jane together in bed crashed around inside my head. My skin felt as though it was crawling whenever I thought about it. It brought me right back to the time I had walked in on Marc with Nadia and that awful sick feeling in the pit of my stomach. I narrowly missed being hit by a bus when I cycled through a red light. The driver blared his horn angrily, and the passengers glared through

90

the windows at me.

When I reached the apartment, I put my key in the lock and let myself in. The place was chilly. Slanted sunbeams filtered in through the glass catching dust motes in its rays. I wasn't used to seeing the place during the daylight hours anymore. It hit me then; I wasn't just losing Sam – I was losing my home too. I felt overwhelmed by the sheer ache in my heart.

When I took my phone out of my pocket I saw I had several missed calls and messages from Sam, but I switched it off without even bothering to read them. I didn't see what words he could possibly offer to explain why Jane had been in his apartment first thing in the morning. When Marc had cheated on me with Nadia, as well as the betrayal, the embarrassment was almost worse. I had been mortified that I was the last person to find out; everyone else had known about them before me. I swore nobody would do that to me ever again. My self-preservation had tightened since Marc, and I had promised myself that I would never again let anyone else put a dent in my armour. I wouldn't listen to any more excuses or lies; I couldn't allow myself to be humiliated any more.

I went into the bedroom, kicked off my shoes, and climbed into bed without bothering to take off my clothes. Our bed. It killed me to think of Sam and Jane together in a different bed over three thousand miles away. I fell asleep and dreamt that Jane and I were contestants on Mastermind and we were both competing for Sam. Sam was the host and he would ask us a question about himself and every time I gave what I thought was the right answer, Jane would trump me with something even

91

better. "But it's me!" I kept protesting when it was clear that I was losing badly, but Sam didn't seem to care. He pressed his hand down on the buzzer.

I woke up in a sweat and opened my eyes. It was dark beyond the blinds. My heart was racing, and it took me a second to get my bearings. I checked the time and saw I had been asleep for six hours. I heard the buzzer again, the same one from my dreams, obnoxious and insistent. I realised it was coming from the door. I pulled back the duvet and put my two feet on the floor before making my way out to the hall. I checked through the peephole to make sure it wasn't an axe murderer, and when I saw Frankie's chaotic hair at the other end, I opened it and let her in.

"What's going on, Lily?" Frankie said, immediately stepping inside. "Are you okay?"

"What do you mean?"

"Your phone is off. I've been trying to call you. I had six missed calls from Sam, so I called him back thinking something awful had happened to you, but he just said you had had a misunderstanding and he asked me to get you to call him back. I've been worried sick!" Frankie said.

"'A misunderstanding,' is that what he called it?" I practically spat the words back at her. She shut the door behind her and made her way over to the sofa.

She raised the palms of her two hands to face me. "Hey, don't shoot the messenger!"

"So I guess he left out the bit about the woman in the background then?" I said, following her over.

92

Her mouth fell open. "What?"

"When I called him back after I was talking to you earlier, I could hear a woman's voice in the background. It was Jane."

"Oh, Lily . . . do you think it could have been innocent? He sounded distraught when I was talking to him."

"Believe me I've wracked my head to see if I could come up with another explanation for what was going on, but it was six a.m. in the morning, what other reason could there be except that they had spent the night together?" Once again the sting of what had happened assailed me. It was like sandpaper being rubbed back and forth across my skin.

"Oh, honey, I'm so sorry!"

I sighed. "I've had my suspicions about the two of them for weeks now."

She sat down onto the sofa and I did the same. I looked around the room so full of Sam's personality that it felt like a stab to the heart once again.

"I'm shocked. I really thought Sam was one of the good ones."

"So did I."

"This calls for wine."

I let Frankie select a bottle from the wine chiller, and she poured us both a glass. "Look, maybe you should talk to him, give him the benefit of the doubt? I know I'm the last person who should be giving advice, but long-distance relationships are tricky –"

"No way!" I shook my head resolutely. "There is no way I'll ever let another man make a fool of me the way Marc did.

93

The first time I can put down to naïvety but to let it happen a second time would be utter stupidity."

CHAPTER 14

We drank the first bottle and then opened another one. Suddenly, I felt panicked about *Baked with Love*. What if Dad had been trying to call me about something and my phone was off? I quickly found it in my handbag and switched it on. Immediately I was assailed with messages notifying me of missed calls from Sam. There were lots of texts too. I was relieved to see there were none from Dad. Fortified by the wine, I decided to read the messages and see what Sam had to say for himself.

The first one was:

"Please call me, Lily, I need to talk to you. I can explain everything."

After that they began to get increasingly more desperate:

"Please call me, Lily – I love you."

Then:

"Please pick up, Lily. You've got this wrong. Jane did stay over but she slept in my room and I stayed on the couch. She was so drunk that I didn't want to send her home on her own. I thought I was doing the right thing by making sure she was okay, but I can see why you would think there is something going on. Call me, please."

I read through them until finally the last one said simply:

"Jane is gay."

I nearly spilled the glass of wine out of my hand. I quickly put it down on the coffee table, causing some of the wine to spill over the rim of the glass. I read it again and then another time to make sure I wasn't imagining it.

"What is it?" Frankie asked, noticing my face.

I passed the phone to her.

"Oh my God," she said open-mouthed.

"How do I know if he's telling the truth?" I whispered.

"Well, maybe you should call him and listen to what he has to say?"

I quickly calculated the time difference. It was midnight in Ireland, so it would be around seven in New York. I took a deep breath and dialled his number. My heart was thumping as I waited for the call to connect.

"Lily!" he answered almost straight away as if he had been sitting with his phone in his hand.

"I just read your message. Jane is gay?"

Sam sighed. "She's in a long-term relationship with a woman. She has no interest in me."

"But why didn't you tell me that before?" I said angrily. "|You could have saved us a lot of hassle here, Sam!"

"Well, you wouldn't answer my calls! You switched your phone off!"

"But before that, when you knew I was going out of my mind with worry about what was going on between you and Jane, why didn't you just put my mind at ease and tell me she was gay?"

"Because part of me is very angry that after all this time

96

together you still don't trust me. I've never given you any reason not to, but all because of that dickhead Marc, I suffer the repercussions! Your trust issues are always causing problems for us, and I thought to myself, why should I have to explain? No matter what I say or do, you believe what you want to believe anyway."

"That's unfair, Sam. I heard another woman in your apartment first thing in the morning! What would you think if the situation had been reversed?"

"I hope I would trust you enough not to let the doubts take over."

"Come on, Sam, all the signs were there! Plus, you know I've been hurt before, it's hard for me . . ."

"I think this distance is driving us both crazy . . ." Sam said resignedly.

I sighed feeling defeated. "This is so hard, Sam."

"I know but you have to trust me – I am not Marc. If you don't trust me, then we can't make it work."

"That's what Frankie said -"

"Well, she's right –"

He paused. "Please trust me, Lily. I promise that I would never do anything to hurt you. My mother raised me to never break a promise – I'm a man of my word." Suddenly, it hit me. I didn't have to be angry any more. In fact, I could be very, very happy. Sam and Jane's relationship was platonic. It felt as though there were a million excited butterflies in my stomach. I couldn't help smiling.

"Oh, Sam, I'm sorry. I'm so sorry for not trusting you. I'm

so happy you weren't having an affair though!"

"I keep telling you I never would, Lily. You're the only woman I want to be with. I love you and only you."

I beamed a smile as wide as the Liffey. "I love you too, Sam. Next time I see you I promise I'll make it up to you!"

"You better!" Sam said, laughing.

Out of the corner of my eye I could see Frankie pretending to vomit. "Okay, enough already! Wrap it up, you two!"

CHAPTER 15

The next morning I busied around the café serving cakes and coffees. The heavenly smell of roasted arabica beans, brown sugar, and scones fresh from the oven filled the air. As winter was now pushing out autumn, I had changed the menu; gone were the lighter-than-air lemon meringue pies and fruit-filled tarts in favour of richer-flavoured cakes, full of body and spice.

The bell tinkled and I saw it was Mabel again, but this time she was alone.

"Good morning, Mabel, no Lottie today?" Dad said raising his head from the till as he spotted her coming through the door. He rushed past me to serve her.

"Morning, Hugh. No, her mum is off work today."

I noticed that she wasn't her usual spritely self; she was normally so bubbly and full of life, but today it was as though she had the weight of the world on her shoulders.

"So how have you been keeping?" Dad asked.

"Oh, I've been better . . ." She began fiddling with the clasp on her handbag.

"I don't mean to pry," Dad said gently, "but is everything okay?"

"It's my husband's fifteen-year anniversary today. I was just at mass there for him. I can't believe he's been gone for that long; it feels like just yesterday that he passed . . . I miss him every day, but some days it hits you harder than others."

Dad nodded his head knowingly. "Well, it's been thirty-three years since I lost my Linda so I know exactly what you mean. It never gets any easier, does it?"

She shook her head sadly. "No, Hugh, it certainly doesn't."

Dad seldom ever mentioned my mum, so when he did it was like a glimpse into his heart. Even after all this time, he still found it difficult to talk about her. When she had died suddenly of a brain aneurysm all those years ago, a part of him had died too that day.

"Sit down there and I'll bring you over something nice," Dad said kindly.

I watched as he made Mabel a pot of tea and carefully chose a slice of my decadent Baileys white chocolate gateau for her. I mentally approved of his selection – everyone knew that chocolate cake had healing powers and the hint of Baileys gave it an extra edge. He brought it over and set the tray down in front of her. I watched as her face broke into a smile. My cake was doing its job once again.

I was in the middle of wiping down a table, and when I looked up, I saw Frankie standing there with a big smile on her face.

"Have you got five?"

I pushed a stray strand of hair back from my forehead. "No, I'm up the walls with customers today."

Frankie looked over at Mabel - an island, surrounded by a sea of empty tables and looked back at me quizzically.

"Joke," I said. "Go on into the kitchen and I'll be with you

100

in a sec."

"You'll never guess what?" she chimed as soon as I came through the door.

"What?" I said, placing down my cloth and antibacterial spray.

"Oh, you're going to love me!" she sang.

"Just tell me, Frankie, jeez!"

"I have just got us two first-class tickets to New York and we leave tomorrow!"

"What?"

"Well, I got asked to style the clothes on a shoot for Siesto make-up, and when I heard it was in New York I chanced my arm and told them I needed an assistant and you're it!"

"But I can't – what about this place?"

"It's only for three days, Lily – two of which you're not even open! Your Dad will keep things ticking over."

"But Friday is my busiest day – I can't – I'm sorry."

"Come on, Lily, it's only for one day – you said yourself the place is dead – it won't fall apart without you. Don't you want to see Sam? I thought you'd be thrilled!"

"Of course I do, but it's not that easy –"

"I'm not taking no for answer. Get everything sorted today because you have a busy weekend ahead of you!"

Then she turned and breezed back through the door as calmly as she had entered, leaving me in a fluster. She was crazy. As much as I'd love to, I had a bakery to run. I couldn't just fly off to New York.

"Excuse me," Dad said, coming into the kitchen a few

minutes later with a pile of crockery and gesturing to where I was standing in front of the dishwasher. I was still in shock from Frankie's visit. I moved to the side and let him stack it.

"How's Frankie?" he asked as if reading my mind.

"You won't believe it –"

"What?" he asked.

"She wants me to go to New York with her. She has a shoot on for the weekend and she's managed to put me down as her assistant."

He lifted his head from his task and smiled. "Oh, Lily, that's fantastic, I hope you said yes?"

"But I can't just walk out and leave you here to run this place on your own!"

"You can't turn down the opportunity to visit Sam!"

Whenever I thought about the chance to see him, I felt overwhelmed with longing. How amazing would it be to turn up on his doorstep and surprise him? It would also give us a chance to put the tensions of the last few weeks behind us and get things properly back on track between us again.

"I'll be fine," Dad continued. "And I'm sure Clara will step in and give me a hand."

"Do you think?" Suddenly, a seed of hope opened up inside me. Perhaps if I left everything ready for him and he had Clara to help, too, they could manage without me for one day?

"You're going, Lily, and I won't hear another word against it. Don't look a gift horse in the mouth!"

I protested some more, but Dad quashed my worries and told me that I was going and that was the end of it. I decided to

102

call Clara next to see if she could help Dad out, there was no point in even entertaining the idea if she wasn't available. I explained everything and although she acted like she was doing me a huge favour, which she was in fairness, I could tell that she was secretly delighted at the chance to get behind the counter of *Baked with Love*. I suspected she had long been waiting for her opportunity to come and have a nose around. No doubt she saw herself as some sort of consultant brought in to look analytically at every aspect of the business and give a critique on my return. I told myself that even listening to a dressing-down from Clara would be worth it if I got to spend a few days with Sam.

After I hung up from her I felt a bubble of excitement fizz up inside of me and I started to laugh – I was actually going to New York. Tomorrow I would be with Sam!

I was in a tizzy for the rest of the day. My head was spinning thinking of all of the things that I needed to do before I left. I worked late into the evening to get things ready to hand over to Dad. I had lists and then when they began to get out of control, I began to make lists of the lists. Then I had to do a master list to keep all the sub-lists in order. I had them pinned up all over the kitchen wall, with arrows directing Dad and Clara where to find things. I had done as much prep as I could for them; I just hoped it would be enough.

After we had closed the door that evening, Clara called over and I sat her and Dad down and talked them through everything. Clara had her head bent as she scribbled furiously into a notebook trying to keep up with my instructions. I was just talking them through my scone recipe when she lowered her pen and raised her hand to stop me mid-sentence.

"So how many sultanas should I use per scone?" she asked.

I looked at her quizzically wondering if she was joking, but I saw she was deadly serious.

"I don't know . . . maybe ten?" I replied.

"Well, how many is it exactly?" she said impatiently.

"It doesn't really matter, Clara."

"Oh, but it does, Lily. They may look tiny but don't be deceived! Each sultana costs you money. If you use fewer sultanas per year, you are spending less on your raw materials, and if you spend less on your raw materials, then you improve your bottom line. You really should be keeping an inventory of your ingredients. It's basic business strategy – you need to start thinking in terms of margin, Lily!" She wagged her pen at me. "It's no wonder the business is struggling!"

I groaned inwardly. I could visualise her counting out the sultanas individually instead of just whacking a load in like I usually did. Patience, I told myself, patience. It would all be worth it. I could put up with Clara and her mad ways because she was doing me a huge favour. "Good point, Clara, go with eight so."

She looked satisfied with this as she wrote it down in her notebook. I could see Dad struggling to keep a laugh inside.

"Now, there's one thing that's very important to me and I need you both to promise me you won't interfere . . ."

"What is it?" Dad asked, his forehead creasing with concern.

"You have to swear to me that you won't mess with my

104

recipes – you have to use real butter," I said, wagging my pen at both of them. I had visions of people eating my cakes while I was gone and not getting that melt in the mouth taste that I took so much pride in.

Clara reddened and I knew she had already planned to substitute the butter with margarine.

"Don't worry," Dad said. "We'll do everything exactly the way you do it, won't we, Clara?"

"Fine," she said, slamming shut her notebook.

"Now you go and have fun with Sam, do you hear me?" Dad warned when I had finished. "We won't burn the place down."

* * *

The next morning I sat in a taxi on my way to the airport with nervous excitement coursing around me. I had never been to New York before, and although it was going to be a very brief trip, my head was full of romantic images involving snowflakes and Christmas decorations just like I had seen in movies. I had visions of taking a carriage around Central Park, strolling hand in hand down Fifth Avenue, maybe even a kiss at the top of the Empire State Building. I hadn't told Sam I was coming. We would be arriving in New York at around lunchtime, so I had planned on rocking up to Sam's office to surprise him. I felt a tingle run through my body at the thoughts of feeling his warm mouth over mine, running my fingers through his wavy, dark hair, the touch of his hands on my skin again. Butterflies charged around chaotically inside my stomach. I only had a few more hours to wait.

105

I met Frankie and, after we had checked in, we headed to the first-class lounge. It was mainly full of business travellers wearing smart suits and other fancy people wearing butter-soft leather loafers and carrying designer handbags. I had worn my best clothes so I would look the part, but I still felt like a total imposter. There were fridges running along one wall that were stocked full of wine and champagne that you could just help yourself to, and a woman was walking around offering free shoulder massages. I would have been happy just to stay in the lounge let alone get on the plane. Frankie insisted we get a glass of bubbles to kick-start our trip.

"But I haven't even had my breakfast yet!" I protested.

"Breakfast, smekfast, we're going to New York, baby!" she said, handing me a flute and we clinked glasses.

It wasn't long before we were called to board. For the first time in my life and probably the last, I got to turn left instead of right on a plane. I couldn't help but squeal when we were shown to our seats.

"Oh my God, this is amazing!" I said, playing with the remote and instantly reclining the seat back into a bed.

"Shhhhh," Frankie hissed. "Act cool."

Then we were given a bag of toiletries. "I can't believe all of this is free!" I gushed as I lifted out a luxury face cream. "How will I ever go back to economy after this?"

The airhostess offered us more free champagne and we were both tipsy before we had even left the tarmac at Dublin Airport.

I slept most of the flight. The champagne coupled with the

106

heavy thrum of the engines had lulled me to sleep. It was only when I felt someone shaking my shoulder that I woke up and saw Frankie's face above me.

"You were snoring like a trooper," she whispered. "I had to intervene for the sake of the other passengers. They were starting to complain."

I noticed a patch of drool on my lovely first-class pillow. I tried to sit myself upright and I pressed the button to retract the seat, but the duvet somehow got tangled in the mechanism and I almost strangled myself.

"Help me, Frankie!" My voice came out muffled under the duvet.

Frankie managed to untangle me from the blanket before convulsing into laughter. When I was free, I sat upright and looked around. The other passengers were glaring at us. I gave them an apologetic smile.

Soon the New York skyline came into view and I was transfixed as I looked out at the city below us. Frankie pointed out the Empire State Building and the gleaming new Freedom Tower, which looked like a sparkling beacon in the horizon. I felt so giddy. This was actually happening, in just a few hours I would be in Sam's strong arms.

As we made our way out to the taxi queue, the New York cold snap was out in force. A biting wind nipped at our exposed faces, and we were glad when we finally sat on the upholstered leather seat of our car. I gave the driver the address of Sam's office and as we hit downtown I couldn't believe the noise and the traffic. There was a constant tooting of horns, it seemed for

107

no reason, and the skyscrapers were so tall that you would have to lie flat on the pavement to see the tops of them. The graceful old buildings were decorated with Christmas swags and garlands, showing off their finery for the holiday season. I could see why people always said that there was nowhere better than a New York Christmas.

"Here you go, Lily," Frankie said when we eventually came to a stop outside the glazed skyscraper where Sam worked. It was almost two p.m., so I was hoping that after I surprised him he would be able leave the office early. Frankie was going straight to work on the shoot.

"Thanks, Frankie, for all of this," I said, my heart beating wildly as I started to climb out of the car.

"Go surprise your man, Lily!"

CHAPTER 16

I got out of the taxi and took my case out of the trunk. I stood and craned my neck to look up at the glass skyscraper on the street in front of me. I was completely awestruck by its height. I walked through the revolving door, which lead to a marble-clad foyer. When I had located the lift, I went inside and was greeted with a panel that had more buttons than I had ever seen before. I pressed the button for the seventy-ninth floor where I knew Sam worked and it began its ascent upwards. When the doors parted, I found myself standing outside the plush offices of First Ireland Bank. Mahogany panelling ran along the walls, and thick carpet was underfoot. My heart was hammering and suddenly a wave of panic assailed me. What if Sam was in the middle of something and he might not be able to see me? I took a deep breath and went up to the reception desk.

"Hello, I'm wondering if I could speak to Sam Waters please?"

"Do you have an appointment?"

"Um, no, it's a personal matter."

"Let me call him and see if he can meet with you, one moment please."

I listened to the one-sided conversation as the receptionist spoke with someone at the other end.

"I'm sorry but Sam is on a vacation day today, he won't

return to the office until Monday morning," she said to me as she put down the phone.

It felt as though my heart had thudded right down as far as the lobby I had just came from. "Do you know where he has gone?" I said feeling floored. I hadn't even entertained the scenario that he might not be here.

"I'm afraid not. I'm sorry."

I felt totally deflated. I knew I could try calling him on his mobile, but I wanted to surprise him in person. I would just have to try his apartment and hope he would be there.

I descended back down in the elevator and exited onto the busy sidewalk. I took out the map I had grabbed in the airport and studied it for a moment. The grid system meant I was able to locate the street where Sam's apartment was easily enough. I counted that it was only six blocks away.

"Hey, lady, move outta the way!" a man said angrily. I looked up and saw people glare at me as they walked around where I was standing smack bang in the middle of one the world's busiest sidewalks.

"Oh, I'm sorry . . ." I said, quickly stepping out of their way before standing in somebody else's path. "Sorry –" I said again. They rolled their eyes at me as I stepped aside. I quickly folded my map back up again and continued to walk down the sidewalk. The streets were swarming with people chatting on their phones, holding coffee to go in their hands. Even though it was still daytime, I couldn't believe how much the streets were shaded from sunlight by the gigantic tower blocks. I had always heard that New York was a loud, brash city but the sheer noise of the traffic, horns, and people was almost overwhelming.

I eventually reached Sam's building. I stepped into the carrara marble clad foyer where a concierge stood behind a desk.

"I'm looking for Sam Waters," I said.

"Let me see if he's in, just one moment please."

I waited as he called up to Sam's apartment and I knew when nobody answered that Sam wasn't at home.

"He's not in, is he?" I groaned.

The man shook his apologetically. "I'm sorry. Do you want me to leave a message for when he returns?"

"It's okay, thanks." I really didn't want to ruin the surprise. I decided I would give him two hours, and if he didn't return by then, I would call him. I hated wasting precious time that could be spent with him, but I had waited this long, a few more hours wouldn't kill me.

I left my case in the luggage store and decided to head to Frankie's shoot to kill some time. It was taking place in an old Chelsea loft. I couldn't believe how easy it was to find my way around the city. I had only been there for a few hours and already I had mastered the grid system. On autopilot I walked downtown passing block after block, stopping at the intersections until the white man flashed that it was safe to cross. White steam clouds rushed up from the manholes just like I had seen in the movies.

I eventually found the building and climbed six flights of stairs until I came to the loft where the shoot was taking place. Frankie had told me that it used to be a clothing factory back in the sixties but had long since been vacant. The original red-

111

bricked walls were left exposed and the wide-plank hardwood floors were stripped bare. Red steel columns broke up the vast space, and pipes and iron beams ran along the ceiling.

"Well?" Frankie asked, hurrying over to me as soon as I came through the door. "How did it go? Where's Sam?"

"He wasn't there, he's on a vacation day," I sighed.

"Oh, Lily, you must be so disappointed. Come here," she said, slinging her arm around me. "Why don't you call him?"

"I really want to see his reaction face-to-face. I'm going to see if he comes back to his place in a few hours, but if he's not back by then, I'll call him."

"Frankie, where are those Alaïa sandals?" a New York accent demanded.

"Sorry, coming now!" she sang.

"Look, I have to get back to work."

I sat down on an old cast-iron radiator and thought about Sam. My biggest worry was that he had left Manhattan for the weekend. Then the whole trip was a massive waste of time. He hadn't mentioned anything about going away anywhere but supposing it had been a spur of the moment thing? What if a few of them had decided to head away at the last minute?

Frankie knocked me out of my thoughts by handing me a steamer.

"You can make yourself useful while you're here. Would you mind steaming these clothes for me – you'd be doing me a huge favour?"

"Sure," I said. "I might as well earn my keep." Once she had shown me what to do, I set to work taking the creases out of

112

the clothes while she chatted with the creative director.

When I was finished with the clothes, I watched as Frankie fitted them on the models. They were beautiful creatures, long and lean with endless limbs. They were all angles; hip bones, jawbones, and collarbones jutted out. I felt like a little round dumpling beside them. Even though the clothes were in the smallest sizes possible, they were still too big for their slender bodies, so I watched as Frankie had to pin them in to fit. They all wore carefully applied make-up, some had theatrical eyeliner or others had heavy-coloured lips.

After a while the creative director signalled a break and lavish amounts of food were brought in to the room. I nearly wet myself when I saw the boxes had the logo of the Ansel Bakery, New York's most famous bakery. People queued from the early hours of the morning just to try out their cronuts and now, tray upon tray of heavenly goodies was being laid out and it was all for free! It was all displayed on a table running the length of the room but after the delivery guy had left, nobody moved to get any. I waited for a few more minutes to be polite. I didn't want to look like a pig, but after ten minutes, it became clear that nobody was going to eat anything, so I went over to the table and picked up a cronut. I had been dying to try one ever since I had first heard about them; half-doughnut, half-croissant, they were the latest craze in the baking world. I thought I had died and gone to heaven as I bit into the sweet coconut-flavoured cream, which was sandwiched between the layers of thin pastry. It had the airiness of a croissant but with the doughy sweetness of a doughnut as the flakes melted in my mouth. It was one of

113

the nicest things I had ever eaten.

"Why is nobody eating this?" I asked Frankie, completely baffled.

She shrugged her shoulders. "It's the same on every shoot I do. Nobody dares to eat anything. It's like a game of competitive non-eating. You get used to it."

"I can't believe none of you –" I swallowed a mouthful, "are going to eat these?" I looked around at all the models in the room in disbelief.

Nobody would make eye contact with me.

"But they're from the Ansel Bakery! People queue from four a.m. in the morning to try them!" I said in dismay.

I noticed Frankie using her fingers to draw a pretend zip across her lips telling me to shut up.

I was definitely going to try my own version in *Baked with Love* when I went back home. Even though I had only been gone for a few hours, I found I missed my bakery. I made me realized just how much I loved working there. I loved that people enjoyed my food; from the moment they tasted it, I could see the expression of pure delight on their faces as they bit into my vanilla cream croissants and a little surprise bit of the custard squeezed out from inside or how an almondy bakewell slice could set a bad day to rights. Or how the tiniest sprinkle of salt perfectly balanced a sweet caramel. I loved being able to give people that experience. Food was one of life's simplest pleasures. Life could be hard and there were enough rough days that we all deserved to indulge in the little treats wherever we could get them. It saddened me that the people here wouldn't allow themselves to do that. I know I had spent so many years dieting in a quest to be skinnier, to look angular like the women here now in front of me, but *Baked with Love* had allowed me to make peace with my body. Food was all about enjoyment. What was better than the bittersweet taste of lemon curd layered thick on buttery shortcrust pastry? The taste lingering in your mouth long after the final bite.

"I can't stay here, it's a complete head-melt," I said to Frankie after a few minutes. I was beginning to feel like a specimen in the zoo as the models watched me open-mouthed when I had eaten yet another cronut.

"But where are you going to go?"

"I'll try Sam's place again, hopefully he might be back now."

"Okay, well, I'll call you the second we wrap up here, okay?"

I grabbed my bag and headed for the door. I risked a last look around the loft where a model was now being pinned into the shimmering dress that I had just steamed. I made my way down the six flights of stairs until I finally came outside onto the pavement.

I headed back uptown towards Sam's building again. As soon as I entered the foyer the concierge shook his head sadly at me.

"I'm afraid he hasn't returned yet," he said before I had a chance to speak. Defeated, I walked back outside onto the sidewalk. I couldn't believe that I was in this city where Sam was too, one of the most romantic cities in the world, and yet we weren't together.

I stood on the pavement and looked up at the sky. "Mam, if you're listening up there, now would be a good time to start cutting me a little bit of slack if you wouldn't mind!"

I noticed passersby looking strangely at me, but I didn't care. I would never see any of them again.

A pigeon flew over my head and I felt something warm and runny fall on my hair. I put my hand up to feel what it was and realised it had come from the pigeon.

"Really, Mam? You are literally shitting on me?" I shouted up to the sky again.

In a temper, I started to walk down the sidewalk and instantly felt myself collide with a hard chest.

"Ouch!" I said rubbing my head. I raised my head and could not believe it when I looked up and saw it was Sam.

CHAPTER 17

"Lily?" he said, pulling back from me.

"That hurt," I said, rubbing my forehead. "I think I might have concussion."

"Oh my God, are you okay? What the hell are you doing here?"

"Surprise!" I said, smiling weakly.

"But what are you doing in New York?"

"Looking for you. Frankie has a shoot here all weekend, so she managed to swing it to bring me along as her assistant."

"I love Frankie!" he said, grabbing me into a hug. "When did you get here? I can't believe it's you!"

"Just after lunch. I called into your office but they told me you had a day off, so then I tried your apartment and you weren't home."

"I'm sorry but why didn't you call me?"

"I wanted to surprise you face-to-face."

"Well, you've certainly done that!" he said, grinning before wrapping his arms around me again. "I can't believe you're standing here. God, I've missed you." He squeezed me against his chest and it felt as though I was in my rightful place. We kissed deeply and passionately as if we were the only ones in the world and not standing on the sidewalk in one of the world's busiest cities.

"Come on," said Sam. "Let's go upstairs."

We re-entered the marble-clad foyer.

"Reunited at last," the concierge said, smiling at the two of us. We grinned back at him.

We took a lift up to the fourteenth floor. Sam put his key in the door and we went inside. Colourful rugs were scattered across honey-coloured herringbone floors. The high ceilings gave the place a light, airy feel. Full-length floor to ceiling windows looked down over the streets below.

"This place is amazing," I said, walking over to look out through them. Sam's apartment was a prime piece of real estate; I couldn't even begin to imagine what it was costing the company. He put his arms around me from behind and began kissing delicately along the nape of my neck. I turned around to face him, our kisses growing more urgent with every passing second. We moved down onto the sofa, and soon he was undressing me. He pulled my top up over my head and then moved to unbuttoning my jeans.

I wriggled out of them as he fumbled with my bra clasp.

"I'll do it," I said, taking over and quickly taking it off.

"Sorry, I'm out of practice," he said breathlessly.

I pulled off his T-shirt next, exposing his broad dark chest. Then I moved down and pulled off his jeans.

He took off my underwear and soon he was inside me. We moved together passionately making up for the time we had been apart.

Afterwards, we lay there exhausted in a tangled mess. My head rested in the crook of his arm as he stroked lazy circles across the skin of my back.

"So how long have I got you for?" Sam asked.

"I leave Sunday night."

He pouted. "That's less than forty-eight hours."

"It's the best I could do." I sighed.

"Well, in that case, come on, we don't have any time to waste."

He moved down and started kissing my chest, moving slow and tender, and soon we were making love again.

CHAPTER 18

Sunlight crept around the corners of the blinds spreading across the floorboards up across the bed until it warmed our naked bodies. We took our time rousing ourselves. I was enjoying having Sam for two days, and I wanted to use every moment to feel him near me.

"I'm starving!" I said eventually when I could no longer ignore the pangs of hunger in my stomach.

"You must really have worked up an appetite," Sam said, winking at me.

I blushed under his gaze.

"How about I show you a real New York breakfast? We should go to the Loeb Boathouse."

"Where's that?"

"Central Park – it's beautiful."

I pulled back the sheets and stretched. I climbed out of bed and walked over and slid my arms into Sam's toweling robe. Then I went over to the window and peeped through the blinds at the views south and west across the New York skyline. I could see the Jersey Shore in the distance. Yellow cabs stood out from the grey on the street below. It really was the stuff of dreams. We showered together and then got dressed to go explore the city.

* * *

We strolled hand in hand through the winter sunshine, and as we reached the park, it was amazing how the city instantly quieted down just a few steps inside the blanket of the trees. Our breath fogged onto the air as we walked. Long-limbed joggers dressed in brightly coloured running gear overtook us, their feet crunching on the frost-tipped grass. A grey squirrel darted across the path. Carol singers sang under the arches, the music reverberating through the low tunnels. Sam led the way and soon the elegant pillars of the boathouse came into view.

I ate a plate of French toast with a decadent banana compote soaked in Grand Marnier while Sam chose the eggs benedict. It was divine. When we were finished, we grabbed hot chocolates to go and strolled around the lake where people were rowing lazily across the water.

We headed up towards Bow Bridge and posed for selfies with the city making the perfect backdrop against the bare trees of the park. We skated in the Wollman Rink, and I laughed as Sam confidently took to the ice only to lose his footing a few steps in and land upended on his bum.

When we were finished, Sam rubbed his hands together to warm himself up from the biting cold. My teeth were chattering; we got cold weather in Ireland, but it never was like this. This type of cold seemed to be carried along on the wind, it cut through to the bone. My feet felt like two blocks of ice inside my trainers. Sam slung his arm around my shoulder. "Come on, let's go get you warmed up. I've a special surprise for you."

We strolled back through Central Park hand in hand until we were standing in front of the steps of The Plaza Hotel.

"We're not going where I think we're going, are we?" I asked, jumping up and down excitedly clapping my hands together.

"Uh-huh. I couldn't let you go home without experiencing afternoon tea at The Plaza."

"But don't you need to book it weeks in advance?"

"I pulled a few strings, don't worry." He placed his hand on the small of my back and led me up the plush, red-carpeted steps. The doorman tipped his hat to us and held the door while we went through into the ornate foyer. I winced at the trainers that I was wearing. My jaw dropped as we stepped over to the mosaic-tiled floor. Light bounced around through the crystal chandelier, reflected off the large mirrors. Gold leaf cornicing ran around the perimeter of the ceiling. We stepped through the Romanesque arched doorway and were in the infamous atrium of the Palm Court. Marble pillars were crowned with a beautiful stained-glass dome. Large potted plants and ceiling-high palm trees gave the room an exotic intimacy. I had always dreamed about coming here. Just the name conjured up the glamour and extravagance of a bygone era. I imagined F. Scott Fitzgerald and Zelda sitting drinking in this very room. I could almost hear the echoes of the debauchery, the wild parties, the decadent displays of wealth rarely seen today. It was incredible to think of the history witnessed between these walls, and yet here I was standing there ready to make my own memories.

The waiter showed us to our table and everything about the setting exuded elegance. It was laid out with delicate china, heavy table linen, and weighty crystal glasses. When our tea

123

stand arrived, my mouth started watering. There were miniature deviled egg sandwiches, prime rib sandwiches, lobster roll, and savouries with all kinds of detail on the bottom tier. There were scones served with lemon-flavoured cream and preserves in the middle, and the top tier was filled with the prettiest cakes I had ever seen. The crème de cassis cheesecake and the rose water macaron were a treat to the senses. It was definitely inspiration for *Baked with Love*.

"This has been the most perfect day," I said to Sam as we linked arms and walked back through the foyer when we were finished.

"I'm just so glad to have you here," he said, squeezing me against him.

Suddenly as we reached the door I noticed plump snowflakes falling gracefully outside. "Oh my God, it's snowing!"

I was awestruck as I stood on the steps and surveyed how the snow had put a spell on the city. It had dampened down the noise and its usual frenetic pace suddenly seemed calmer. "Pinch me because this is the stuff of fairytales."

"I ordered the weather especially," Sam said, laughing.

We stood and kissed, and I felt as though I was the star in one of the romantic movies that I loved watching. When we pulled away I noticed Sam's face grow serious. Urgent.

"Marry me, Lily –"

"What?" I said. I wasn't sure I had heard him right.

"Lily, marry me. It's perfect – this moment – you're perfect. I'm sorry. I know I'm doing this all wrong – it wasn't meant to be like this." He hurriedly got down on one knee. "I have no ring and I haven't even asked your Dad yet . . . but we've had the most perfect day and I can only see you in my future. I know it's you – it's always been you. I want to spend the rest of my life with you."

I was utterly gobsmacked. I had not expected this.

My face obviously told Sam this. "Say something, Lily," he pressed gently.

"I'm sorry, Sam, it's just such a shock –" I said in a small voice.

"A good one, I hope," he said nervously.

"Of course," I smiled. "I just can't believe it . . ."

"Say yes, Lily –"

I was completely stunned. "Yes, Sam – of course I will marry you." I started to laugh then and he laughed too.

"I love you, Lily. You've made me the happiest man alive. At least this way the distance between us will be a little more bearable for the next few months."

We forgot the world around us as we kissed tenderly on the steps of The Plaza.

CHAPTER 19

The next morning I opened my eyes and saw that it was just before seven a.m. Sam turned around and took me into his arms. "Good morning, fiancée."

Everything that had happened the previous evening came rushing back to me. I couldn't believe we were engaged.

I smiled. "Good morning." My head felt a little tender. We had ended up returning to The Plaza where they had treated us to a complimentary bottle of champagne. Then we had ordered another for good measure.

"Thanks for making me the happiest man alive. There's just one thing though –"

"What?"

"I'm doing this arseways," he groaned.

"What is it?"

"You've no ring –"

"There's no rush, we can get it when you're back home." I folded my arm around his waist and laid my head against his chest. There was no forgetting that I was leaving in a few hours' time and I was dreading the distance between us again.

"No way!" Sam said, sitting upright in the bed and jerking me up with him. "I'm not letting you go home without a ring; it wouldn't be right. I want the world to know that you're mine."

"Okay," I said, laughing as he hopped out of bed eagerly.

"Come on, there's only one place we can go in this city."

* * *

As we strolled down Fifth Avenue, I took in the twinkling fairy lights and wreaths on every building. We stopped to watch the famous light show on the walls of Saks and then went to see the colourful fairy lights twinkling on the seventy-foot tree at the Rockefeller Plaza. I couldn't help but feel the whole city was wrapped up like a giant Christmas present. I could see why people loved New York. There was an excited energy; the streets were thronged with shoppers, people were jubilant, and it was hard not to get caught up in the festive atmosphere.

Sam held my hand firmly as we snaked our way through the crowds. Soon I could see Tiffany & Co in the distance and I realised that was where we were going. When we neared the door, a couple emerged hand in hand, both beaming. They stopped and looked down at her left hand giggling, and I saw a beautiful engagement ring stood proudly on her ring finger. I smiled at them. I could not believe I was getting my engagement ring there too.

We walked through the art deco showrooms and made our way to the diamond rings. We peered through the endless glass displays of stunning jewellery. How on Earth was I supposed to choose?

"Can I help you there?" a salesman greeted us.

"We've just got engaged!" Sam said proudly.

"Congratulations! An engagement ring from Tiffany's is a symbol of true love and a lifetime of commitment. Its brilliance signifies the promise of a long future together," he said.

128

Suddenly I felt my stomach lurch. The words "lifetime of commitment" felt like an assault. I thought of the last time I had chosen an engagement ring; I had thought I was getting a lifetime commitment then too. I took a deep breath and tried to quash those thoughts; I didn't want bad memories to ruin what was happening right now. I had to keep reminding myself that Sam wasn't Marc.

The salesman lifted out cushioned trays of diamonds and I tried on ring after ring.

"What about this one?" the salesman suggested, taking out an emerald cut diamond. "The elegant cut of the centre stone is embraced by bead cut diamonds all set on a platinum band."

I slipped the ring up my finger, and I held my hand out to admire it. The light caught the dazzling centre stone beautifully. I wished I had been born with naturally slender, elegant digits rather than my chubby little stumps, but it was stunning. I knew it was the one.

We left Tiffany & Co a while later and I was swinging a little blue bag even though it was empty as I already had the ring on my finger, but I couldn't bear not to take a bag with me anyway. Whenever I caught a glimpse of the ring's sparkle, I kept stopping to admire it; even on my stumpy fingers, it still looked dazzling. I had stripped off the rings Marc had given me after I had found him in bed with Nadia, and I'd forgotten how much I had loved wearing them.

By the time we had left Tiffany & Co it was time to go back to Sam's so I could start packing to leave. My heart filled with heaviness. I had been dreading this bit. I had been trying not to let my impending departure overshadow the last few hours we had together, so I had blocked it out of my head, but now that the time was upon us I had to face up to reality. It would be several more months before we would see each other again, and the time together had been so sweet that it was going to be all the more difficult to be apart again.

"I wish I could magic a way for us to be together." I sighed as I put my clothes back into my case. It felt like just minutes ago that I was packing to come here and now I was heading back home.

"Me too," Sam said dolefully.

Frankie had ordered a car to pick me up at three p.m., and every time I looked at my watch to check the time, I felt the weight of gloom.

"Taxi's here," I said eventually when Frankie called to say that the car was downstairs.

Sam walked me down to the street. I saw Frankie waving to us from the backseat of the cab. Sam pulled me in close to his chest, and I felt tears building in my eyes. He tilted my face up towards his and kissed me as people busied all around us.

"It's only a few more months and then we're going to be together for the rest of our lives," Sam said, trying to cheer me up.

"I know," I whispered.

The driver sat on the horn to hurry me on, so we reluctantly pulled away from one another and I climbed into the backseat of the car. Sam shut the door after me and I watched as he brought his fingers up to his lips, kissed them, then raised them towards me as the car pulled out into the New York traffic.

CHAPTER 20

I watched from the rearview window until Sam faded to a blur in the New York street, then I turned around and slumped back into the seat.

"Oh my God, Lily! What is that?" Frankie squealed, grabbing hold of my hand. "Is it what I think it is?"

"Uh-huh." I nodded.

"I can't believe it! Congratulations!" She reached across and hugged me hard. "Why didn't you call me?"

"It only happened last night – I'm still getting used to it myself . . ."

"Lily, what is wrong with you? You don't sound like someone who has just got engaged!"

"Of course I am, Frankie. I've just said goodbye to Sam, so excuse me if I'm not doing a Tom Cruise and jumping on the couch –"

"Jeez, Lily, some people have to wait a lifetime for a proposal and you get two before the age of thirty-five. Cheer up."

"Frankie, I'm over the moon, honestly."

She looked at me skeptically.

"Stop it!" I said, getting annoyed with her.

"Sorry," she said after a minute. "I get that you're missing him."

"S'okay."

I turned and looked out the window for the rest of the journey to the airport. The city became flatter, the streets less crowded the farther away we moved from Manhattan. I was already missing Sam intensely. Every time I caught sight of the magnificent diamond on my left hand, it would stir up the sense of loss again.

We were more subdued on the way home compared to the outbound flight. I passed on the free champagne, once we landed in Dublin I would be heading straight to *Baked with Love* so I wanted a clear head. Frankie looked at me in wonderment as she took my glass and her own too.

I put the seat back into the recline position, pulled my duvet up around me, and slept for the whole flight home.

We touched down in Dublin, and the taxi dropped Frankie off at her place while I headed straight to my bakery. I knew I would be busy; Mondays always were as I prepped for the week ahead and having been missing in action the previous Friday would only mean more work for me to catch up on.

I was dying to see how Dad and Clara had got on in my absence. The bell gave its soothing trrring as I let myself in, and I instantly felt my body relax. Even though I had only been gone for three days, it was good to be home; I had missed this place. I looked around the café and was relieved to see that the place was immaculate, exactly the same as I would leave it. I breathed out a sigh of relief. I knew Dad and Clara had done a good job while I was away. I went through to the kitchen and saw everything looked neat and orderly. A little too orderly. I noticed the jars were all arranged by descending height for a start. There were also large signs stuck onto the wall. One said, "Work Station A," there was a "Work Station B" too and another said, "Wash-up Area." I groaned. I knew Clara wouldn't have been able to resist interfering. I went over and pulled them down from the wall where she had Blu-Tacked them on. I realized how attached I had become to my kitchen; I hated anyone messing with it.

Just after eight I was busy pulling out ingredients to get started on the day's baking when I heard my phone go. I quickly removed my latex gloves and saw it was Sam's sister Marita.

"Congratulations!" she sung down the phone to me before I even had time to say hello. "Welcome to the family, I've always wanted to have a sister!"

Sam didn't hang about sharing the news, I thought to myself. "Thanks, Marita. It was such a surprise!"

"It is just the best news ever! We are going to have so much fun planning this wedding! So when do you think it will be? Summer? Winter?"

"I'm not sure yet, it's all been such a whirlwind . . ."

"Well, don't leave it too long, I hate long engagements, it takes all the excitement out of it!"

"I have to talk to Sam . . . we've lots to discuss."

After I had hung up from her, Dad came in.

"Great to see you back, Lily. You see I told you we'd survive without you!"

"You did great, Dad. Thank you – although those signs in the kitchen –"

"Ah yes, I meant to warn you about them . . . you know

what Clara is like . . ."

"Don't worry, I've already taken them down."

Dad laughed.

"Also, have you seen the vanilla pods?" I kept looking for ingredients in their usual spot but couldn't find them.

"I think Clara might have moved the jar somewhere; she was doing something with them there on Friday – she said she was sorting it out for you."

I turned back and looked again at the shelves. I realised that Clara had alphabetised all my ingredients. The jars were all facing forward and labelled neatly.

"She couldn't help herself," Dad said, smiling apologetically.

I laughed. "Well, I suppose I got away lightly if that's all she did."

"I take it you haven't seen the freezer then yet . . ."

I shook my head.

"So how was the weekend?" he asked. "How's Sam?"

"It was amazing, Sam is great – he got such a shock. We had such a good time though. The time flew so we didn't get to do half the things I thought we would, but we went to Central Park and we had afternoon tea at The Plaza." I felt a longing to be with him. It was hard to believe that less than twenty-four hours ago I was lying in his bed in New York. "You'll never guess what else happened . . ."

Dad's eyebrows shot up to his hairline. "What?"

"Sam proposed!" I held out my left hand tentatively to show him the ring.

"Lily, that is wonderful news! Congratulations!" He clasped hold of my hand to admire it.

"So now not only do you have your own bakery but you have a wedding to plan too! I'm so glad things are finally going your way," Dad said after we had sat down with a cup of tea while I filled him in on the proposal. "You deserve it after all you've been through over the last few years."

There they were again, more reminders of my history with Marc. It seemed my engagement to Sam had stirred up all those old hurts once more. It was like I had taken a stick to the bottom of a clear puddle, mixed it all around causing the water to turn dirty brown. It had unsettled everything. I pulled the corners of my mouth upwards in a smile. "Yeah, isn't it great?" I said.

Clara came in later. She had Jacob and Joshua with her. "Hi boys, good to see you! Would you like a honey cookie?" I said.

Their faces lit up. "Yes, please, Auntie Lily!"

Clara was looking at me like I had just offered them heroin. She immediately swiped the cookies out of my hand. "You know they only get treats on Fridays."

They shrugged their shoulders and ran off past me into the kitchen. Out of the corner of my eye I could see Jacob giving Joshua a leg up onto the countertop whereupon he quickly lifted my jar of marshmallows down and handed it to his older brother before jumping down onto the floor beside him. Jacob prised the lid open and stuck his hand deep inside the jar and began stuffing fistfuls of them into his mouth. They were a dangerous duo. I tried to keep a straight face as Clara launched into a spiel

137

about the dangers of sugar.

"Thanks for looking after the place so well while I was away," I said when she eventually was finished ranting.

"Don't mention it, I'd say you'll notice I've implemented a few improvements –"

"Yeah, thanks, they're great," I lied. She walked past me and went straight into the kitchen. The boys quickly hid the jar of marshmallows. She stood with her hands on her hips and surveyed the room.

"Erm, where are my signs gone, Lily?"

"Oh, I thought they were such a good addition that I've ordered permanent ones be printed up," I said quickly. I knew it would be a long time before she stood in this kitchen again and I hoped she would have forgotten all about them by that stage.

She nodded self-satisfactorily. "They are rather good," she said. "A moment of inspired genius!"

"Lily has some good news," Dad said, following us into the kitchen.

"What?" Clara asked, looking at me for answers.

"Sam proposed while I was away."

Her jaw dropped, and it was hard to tell if her reaction to the news was good or bad. "Well, I guess I should say a cautious congratulations, after all, we have been here before with you . . ."

"Now, Clara -" Dad said warningly.

"I'm just being honest, Dad. Don't tell me you're not thinking it too!" She wagged her finger at him, and then turned back to me. "Just try not to mess it up this time."

"I'll do my best," I said through gritted teeth.

* * *

When I had finally finished up that evening, I got a taxi home because I didn't have my bike with me, and besides, my legs wouldn't have been able to cycle even if I had wanted to. I was exhausted, flying through the night and then launching straight back into a full day with *Baked with Love* had wiped me out.

I put my key in the door and let myself into the apartment. I wheeled my case inside and flopped down on the sofa. The place was chilly having been left unoccupied all weekend. I hated being here on my own. Our home lacked its heart when Sam wasn't there.

I opened up my laptop and clicked on Skype. I dialled Sam's number and I watched as the grainy image became clearer and Sam materialised on the screen in front of me. He was sitting in his office, dressed in a shirt and tie, and looking incredibly handsome.

"So how was your first day back, fiancée – I love being able to call you that –" he said.

"Well, *Baked with Love* survived without me so that's good."

"Have you started telling people the good news yet?"

"Well, just Dad and Clara . . . oh and Frankie too of course. I was so busy today, I haven't really had a chance yet . . ."

"Mum and Marita are so excited. They want to know if we'll go black tie or less formal."

"Jeez, they're eager."

He laughed. "They probably thought no woman in her right

139

mind would marry me so they want us to get a move on up to the altar now before you change your mind."

I laughed.

"Look, I have to run to a meeting, but I love you and can't wait to make you my wife."

After I hung up I sat there looking around the room. I was waiting for the excitement to hit me, but nothing was coming and I didn't understand why. I couldn't figure out what was wrong with me. I was exhausted from the weekend, but it was more than that. I should have been ecstatic. I just didn't get it. Why was everyone else far more excited about Sam's proposal than I was? I wasn't even sure myself, but all I knew was that I was pretty sure when you got engaged to someone you weren't meant to feel like this. When Marc had proposed to me I had been over the moon. It had taken me weeks to come back down to Earth. But now I was a world away from that feeling. Maybe it was because it was my second time to get engaged, things were never as good the second time around. Were they?

CHAPTER 21

The next morning I headed into the bakery breathing in the cool morning air of the city deep into my lungs. It was my favourite time of the day, everything was calm, still, and sleepy, and I could be alone with my thoughts before the demands of the day took over. I stopped to let a beeping van reverse into a street before going on again. A jogger passed me in long, elegant strides, puffing white clouds into the air in front of him.

Baked with Love looked so pretty bathed in the low winter sun. It was going to be a glorious December day. I set to work loading up the ovens.

Dad came in soon after and began turning out the scones to cool on the wire rack.

"So, have you come back down to Earth yet?" Dad asked. "I hope you don't mind that I told a few of your aunts and uncles and some of my friends in the golf club. They're all thrilled for you!"

"At least somebody is!" I said, thinking back to Clara's reaction the day before.

"Never mind what Clara said, you know what she's like."

"You think at this stage I'd be used to her, but she still manages to shock me sometimes."

"Well, I'm delighted for you both, Lily. I think you and Sam will be very happy together."

"He called me last night; he's really excited."

Dad cocked his head to the side and looked at me quizzically. "And you are too, aren't you?" he asked.

"Of course . . ."

"Lily, I'm long enough in the tooth to know when something's up. Come on, spit it out –"

"Oh, Dad," I sighed, collapsing down onto a chair. "I just don't know what's wrong with me, but I'm pretty sure this isn't how you're supposed to feel after the man you love asks you to marry him –"

"I'll make us a cuppa," he said calmly. He busied himself making two mugs of tea before sliding one across the small table towards me when he was finished. "There, get that into you," he said. "Now are you going to tell me what's going on?"

"I just don't know, Dad . . ." I said, clasping the mug between my hands. "I mean, I should be excited – I have just got engaged, so I don't know why I'm not. When Marc proposed, I couldn't sleep for weeks afterwards just thinking about it all. I was so excited!"

"Sure, I remember it well. I thought you'd taken leave of your senses completely!" He smiled kindly at me.

"But I don't know . . . I just don't feel the same way this time."

"Well, you're probably a bit more cautious now after everything that happened with Marc. There's nothing wrong with that."

"But what if that means that Sam is not the one for me, Dad?" I blurted. "I don't want to have another marriage go down

142

the toilet!"

"Hey now, Lily, you and Sam are great together. It's just nerves – sure that's normal after everything you've been through with Marc. You've a lot going on with the business too, you're probably just feeling a bit . . . overwhelmed."

"Do you think, Dad?"

"I know, Lily. Now come on, we're going to have hungry customers coming through the door in five minutes. Let's get a move on."

I stood up from the table and started to get on with the day. Soon I was so busy immersed in the work that I loved that I wasn't fretting about Sam.

CHAPTER 22

The next few weeks went by in a blur of Christmas preparations. I did everything I could to inject a bit of festive atmosphere into *Baked with Love*. I lit the stove first thing every morning so that it was always cosy and inviting. I had strewn Christmas decorations across the ceiling. I had used tinned snow to make it look as though the windows were frosted. I made little cake pops in the shape of reindeer heads or star-shaped mince pies, but nothing I did seemed to make a difference. It was so disheartening. Business was still far too slow. Some days, it seemed like it was picking up but other days, especially if the weather was bad, it felt practically empty. The new Starbucks had opened, and every time I passed by, it seemed to be thronged. It was full of cool, young hipsters clicking away on laptops. It made me wonder if maybe I had got my business model all wrong? Maybe people didn't want somewhere to go and relax. Maybe they didn't want somewhere homely; maybe they just wanted the convenience of getting their coffee quickly and being able to get some work done in peace. Maybe nobody cared about lovingly crafted pastries. But then when I thought of my small band of loyal customers, people like Mabel and her granddaughter Lottie - I knew they loved this place almost as much as I did. They had become regulars and Mabel and Dad seemed to have struck up a friendship. Every time they came in, while Lottie was dreamily swirling a chocolate spoon through warm milk and biting down on a honey cookie, he would stop by the table and they would have a little chat.

Sam was almost halfway through the secondment now so it seemed like the worst was over us. We both missed each other like crazy but I still felt a sense of anxiety whenever he mentioned the wedding though. I had hoped that after a few weeks of being engaged that I would have grown used to the idea, maybe started to feel excitement about planning a wedding, but every time somebody mentioned the "w" word to me, my heart started racing and I would feel a pain deep in the centre of my chest like the weight of the world was compressed against it. All I could think about was my last engagement – Sam's proposal had dredged up so many memories and it hurt as much reliving them today as it did when Marc had left me. I was sure I loved him, but I just couldn't figure out what was wrong with me. All I knew was that this feeling wasn't right.

Sam wouldn't be able to make it home for Christmas. I had been so disappointed when he had told me. He and Jane had to be back in the office the day after Christmas day so he wouldn't have any time off. Jane had invited him over to spend Christmas day with her and her partner Lisa who was flying in for Christmas, so at least he wouldn't be alone. I still cringed every time I thought about how I had accused Sam of sleeping with her.

I was going to spend Christmas at Clara's house and I was already dreading it. I knew she would waste no time getting a dig in at me about the fact that *Baked with Love* was struggling,

146

and I was in no humour for her antics.

I was just taking the batch of gingerbread men out of the oven when Clara blustered in through the kitchen door. I had decided to run gingerbread-decorating workshops in the run-up to Christmas and today was the first day. I thought children might enjoy them and it would give the parents a chance to have a hot mug of coffee and maybe a little treat in peace. I had pots of icing, bowls of chocolate chips and jellies to decorate the face, and Smarties to use for the buttons. I was a bundle of nerves wondering if anyone would turn up. I had printed up fliers and put signs in the window. I hoped it might encourage the mothers I saw walking past pushing their buggies with their Starbucks coffees to go to take a chance on *Baked with Love*. Mabel had taken a stack of fliers with her the last time she was in and promised she'd hand them out at Lottie's music class.

"Hi Clara, how're things?" I asked setting the tray down. I noticed that her face was red and her eyes pink. Her usually perfect blow-dried hair hung limply around her face. Dad followed quickly in behind her. "What is it? Are the kids okay?" I said, taking in her disheveled appearance.

She nodded before convulsing into tears. Dad's face creased in worry. I quickly ushered her to sit down on a chair.

"Oh, Lily –" she sobbed.

"I'll make tea," Dad said.

"Tea isn't going to fix this, Dad!" Clara wailed.

"Clara, please tell me what's going on!" I was beginning to panic. Clara never lost her composure.

She looked up at me, her eyes full of hurt and despair. "It's

Tom – he's having an affair!"

I'm embarrassed to say that I laughed. I know it wasn't the most appropriate reaction to my sister telling me that her husband was having an affair, but Clara had this all wrong. Tom was the least likely man to have an affair.

"Now, come on, Clara, I really don't think that's true – Tom loves you," I said, coming over and putting my arm around her.

She shook her head. "I found the proof, Lily – with my own eyes. I found underwear in our bed when I came home from the PTA meeting last night."

My hands flew up to my mouth. This sounded chillingly familiar. I had found Marc in bed with Nadia, but Tom wasn't like Marc, Tom was well . . . Tom.

"Oh, Clara – no! Are you sure they're not yours?"

Dad looked mortified. "I'll . . . eh . . . just keep an eye out here," he said eager to escape the kitchen.

"Please, Lily," she spat. "I have taste – these were hideous – red . . . polyester – awful things that would be liable to give you a fungal infection down there. He's been working late too. I suppose I've just been so busy with the boys and helping you out here that I wasn't paying him as much attention as I should have been so he decided to run off into the arms of another woman." Her whole body crumpled as more tears spilled down her face.

"Oh, Clara, I'm sorry." I didn't think now was the time to point out that it was only for one day that she helped me out in *Baked with Love*.

"I can't believe he would do it in our house – in our own

bed of all places! Oh, it's just disgusting." She dissolved into tears again. I found a paper napkin and handed it to her to dry her eyes.

"Have you confronted him?"

She shook her head. "It's just been such a shock – I need time to gather myself together before I do anything. I need to work out what my next move will be." She dabbed at the corners of her eyes with the napkin.

It sounded as though she was playing a game of chess rather than dealing with her husband's infidelity.

"You need to talk to him, Clara, find out exactly what happened." I remembered how hurt I had felt when I had found Marc in bed with Nadia, I was reeling with the shock and I wasn't thinking straight for months afterwards, but her situation was different to mine – they had two children together. Clara was angry now, but playing games wasn't going to help anyone. She needed to be honest with Tom and perhaps they could work things out for the sake of Jacob and Joshua.

"Tom is a wealthy man, very wealthy. He's also clever. I've read about these sorts of men, they have money squirrelled away in places you wouldn't believe – offshore accounts, share options, you name it, they have it. They have their exit strategy all planned. Well, I'm going to be one step ahead of him. I'm not going to go rushing in and give all my cards away, no, I'm going to play the long game. I'm going to do some surveillance on him first –" she paused and raised her head to look me straight in the eye, "and then I'm going to ruin him." I actually felt frightened for Tom. Clara would make a formidable opponent. I would never, ever cross her.

"Oh, Clara, just take it one step at a time. You have two children together. You need to talk to him first and hear his side of the story."

"There is only one side in this story – mine. I've given Tom everything – I've sacrificed my career, I have put all my energy into raising our two boys as wonderful human beings. I run a lovely home, I cook nutritious food for us all, and this is how he repays me? He has taken my best years and traded them in for a bit of jiggy with some slapper who should know better. The boys need to be provided for; I have to do it for them."

"But things might get really nasty if you go snooping through Tom's affairs. If this is the end, you don't want to have an acrimonious break-up; it'll be awful for you and Tom but even worse for the boys. You need to work it out with him first - see if you can salvage your marriage . . . go to counselling. It doesn't have to be over –"

"Oh yes, it does - nobody deceives me."

"So what's your next step?"

"I've already hired a forensic accountant to investigate his transactions."

"Be careful, Clara," I warned. "This could get really messy."

She pursed her lips together. "As the saying goes 'hell hath no fury like a woman scorned,' and Tom will rue the day he ever crossed me."

CHAPTER 23

Clara was a woman on a mission; she forensically checked Tom's phone records and then scoured his home office for clues. When that turned up nothing, she looked for bills for a second phone. She even searched his car to see if she could find evidence of his affair.

Her accountant had reported back on Tom's finances, which turned up a very large sum of money sequestered in an account in the Bahamas that Clara hadn't known about. This she reckoned was proof that he was living a double life; it was all the evidence she needed. I had asked her whether she was going to confront him now that she had unrooted his finances, but she had looked at me with a glint of madness in her eyes.

"Oh no, Lily," she said, shaking her head. "I've only just begun. By the time I'm done, Tom will wish he had never looked twice at the red-knickered tramp!"

Dad and I still couldn't believe Tom would do something like that – this was Tom we were talking about – the most mild-mannered, patient man in Ireland. In fact, he always seemed kind of afraid of Clara. I couldn't even imagine where he would have got the balls to conduct an extramarital relationship. Dad had asked Clara several times if she was sure they were knickers she had found and not a bit that had fallen off one of the Christmas garlands that were lavishly draped around her house. I thought that was a stretch myself, but I knew what Dad meant, Tom was the last person I would have expected to have an affair, but it just shows – it's always the ones that you least suspect.

It was three days before Christmas and I was standing at the coffee machine as it hissed air into the milk when a voice from behind me said, "Surprise!"

I swung around and could not believe it when I saw Sam was standing there in front of me.

"Oh my God!" I said, throwing down the jug. "How did you get here?"

"It's been so hard not to tell you, but I wanted it to be a surprise. Did you really think I'd let you spend Christmas without me?"

"Oh, Sam! This is just amazing." Tears filled my eyes and I ran around from behind the counter and flung my arms around his neck. "Come into the kitchen."

We ran in and embraced again. I needed to touch him to make sure he really was here and that it wasn't just a dream. Dad's head swung around from bench. "Sam? What the hell are you doing here?" he said, grinning. He walked over and clapped him on the back. "Welcome home!"

"Christmas isn't Christmas without the people we love," Sam said, beaming at me.

"You auld romantic you!" Dad said. "So how long will you be here for?"

"I leave again on the twenty-eighth, but I'm not even going to think about that now."

"I just can't believe you're here!" I said, squeezing him.

Just then the oven beeped. "Hang on a sec," I said, peeling myself off him and sticking on some oven gloves. "I'd better take these out now or they'll burn. They're for the workshop later."

Soon the air was filled with the festive aroma of ginger. As I whizzed around the kitchen busily prepping for the workshop, I kept stopping to stare at him, afraid he was going to disappear again. Sam chatted excitedly about all the things we could do now that we would be spending Christmas together.

"Sorry, can I get into that cupboard behind you there?"

He stepped to the side out of my way.

"Thanks," I said. "Actually, I need to get into this one now." He moved aside again.

"I'm getting in your way, aren't I?"

"No, of course not," I lied. "I wish I didn't have to work," I sighed and laid my head against his chest. It felt so good to have him physically here.

"Hey, don't worry," he said, wrapping me into his arms. "I knew you wouldn't be able to just drop everything and hang out with me. I've some shopping to do anyway."

"Well, once I close the doors of this place on Christmas Eve, I promise I'll make it up to you." I reached up and planted a kiss on his lips. "We're going to have the best Christmas ever!"

CHAPTER 24

After Dad had gone home that evening, I went into the kitchen and made up the mixtures for the following day's bakes. I tried to work as fast as I could but it was still after nine when I finally got home. I hopped on my bike and hurried home through the city streets, excited to know that instead of going back to an empty apartment, Sam would be waiting for me.

When I came through the door, the hearty smell of a rich casserole greeted me and music was playing softly. The lights were dimmed, and the table was set for two. Tea lights flicked inside their glass holders where Sam had scattered them around the room. "This is gorgeous, Sam. The food smells divine!" I said, getting the rich smell of whatever was bubbling on the hob.

"It's coq au vin."

"Mmmh!"

"You're worth it, fiancée." He handed me a glass of champagne, and we clinked glasses and sat down.

"It's so nice not to be coming home to a cold, empty apartment," I said as he wrapped his arms around me.

"So how was your day?"

"Well, I had a few more kids at the gingerbread workshop today so I guess word of mouth is spreading . . . slowly." I sighed heavily. I had been hoping to get between fifteen and twenty children at each class, but I was a long way off. I knew these things took time to catch on. But how much time? It seemed I was giving it my all and everything I did to try and bring customers in through the door never really took off.

"There's still a few more days left. I bet you'll soon be turning people away."

"I love your optimism." Sam reminded me of Dad; whenever I was anxious about something they both knew just the right thing to say to keep me steady. It was one of my favourite things about him.

"So while you were at work, I thought I'd start looking up some venues and I found this amazing castle just outside of Dublin. You should see it, Lily. I think it would be perfect. I hope you don't mind but I made an appointment to go to look at it over Christmas."

I felt my heart start up again. "That sounds great, thanks, Sam." I forced myself to sound bright.

"Well, don't you want to see what it's like?" he asked.

"Sure, you can show me later."

"What's wrong, Lily?"

"Nothing." I smiled at him.

"If you'd prefer something more modern, I saw this cool hotel in Cork. It's set up on the cliffs – the views would be amazing. We could have a look there instead?" He reached over and took my hand. "All I want is to marry you, it really doesn't matter to me where we do it."

"The castle sounds great. I'm sure I'll love it."

After dinner we sat down on the sofa and finished off the rest of the champagne. Sam pulled out the laptop to show me the castle. It really was stunning.

"See here," he said, showing me an image of a smiling couple with their guests standing on the lawn in the sunshine. "If it was a sunny day, you could even have your drinks reception in the garden!"

"It looks great."

"So do you think we should go with summer then?"

"Yeah, I don't mind."

"Well, we could do winter either? Imagine all the open fires and drinking mulled wine . . . wouldn't that be great?"

I smiled at his enthusiasm. When I had been planning my wedding to Marc, I would have killed for him to have had this much interest in it all.

"What is it, Lily? You don't seem very excited." His forehead creased down in a v between his eyebrows.

"Of course, I am." I started fingering a stray thread on my top. "I'm just tired."

"You're right. I keep forgetting that while I might be on holidays, you're working flat out. We'll leave the wedding planning for tonight," he said, putting away his laptop and taking me into his arms.

* * *

When I went to bed that night, I didn't sleep. I was lying in the crook of Sam's arm, listening to his gentle snoring noises. My stomach was churning in a knot of anxiety.

Eventually as day broke across the city and it began to come to life in a blare of horns and engines, I pulled back the duvet and crept out of bed so as not to disturb him. I padded out to the kitchen and pressed the button on the coffee machine. As I made myself a coffee I thought it all through. When he had surprised me by turning up in *Baked with Love* earlier, I had been elated. Surely if my feelings had changed towards him, I wouldn't have felt like that? I was sure he was the one for me and that I wanted to spend the rest of my life with him, wasn't I? So I couldn't understand, why was I feeling like this?

Not long afterwards I felt Sam's arms wrap me from behind. I jumped.

"You scared me. I didn't hear you getting up."

"Oh sorry," he said, pulling back. He was just wearing his boxer shorts, and his hair was tousled from sleep. "So what has you up so early?"

"I couldn't sleep."

"I hope I wasn't snoring?"

"No, I've just loads to do for work today and my mind was racing."

"I hate it when you're stressed, come back to bed with me." He tugged playfully on my arm. He was smiling at me in that way he had where his eyes twinkled.

"I'm sorry, Sam, I need to get going. I've so much to do before I open up." I couldn't meet his eyes.

"No worries," he said, but I knew he was hurt.

"Sam –"

"It's fine, Lily." He dropped his arms from around my waist and headed back into the bedroom.

CHAPTER 25

I was busy the following morning in *Baked with Love*. I had made Christmas pudding shaped cake-pops and displayed them on a stand inside the windows. People were stopping to admire them, and I was so happy to see some even came inside to buy some. The morning went past in a blur, making frothy hot chocolates and serving Christmassy treats and I was glad that I didn't have too much time on my hands to think about Sam.

The bell tinkled and Mabel came through the door with little Lottie.

"So, what have you got for me today?" she said, rubbing her hands together gleefully. "I must say my mouth has been watering the whole walk down here just thinking about what you might have in store for me!"

"How about this lightly spiced peach and honey cake?" Dad suggested.

"Oooh, that sounds divine, I'll have a slice of that please and a cuppa thanks, Hugh."

"And honey cookie for Lottie," Lottie said.

"Of course, sweetheart," I said, smiling down at her pink cheeks.

"My diet will be out the window," Mabel said, patting her tummy while Dad was serving her.

"Diet?" Dad scoffed. "A woman like you doesn't need to

diet!"

I looked at Mabel, then back to Dad again. They were grinning at one another. Was I imagining it or was Dad flirting? I watched in amusement as he helped her down with her tray.

"I'll have a latte please," I heard the next customer in the queue say distracting me from watching Dad. When I looked up, I saw that it was Sam with a big grin on his face. I was relieved to see that the tensions of that morning seemed to have been forgotten.

"Well this is a nice surprise, what are you doing here?"

"I thought I'd sample this fine new bakery; I hear a hot girl runs it."

I smiled. "Flattery will get you everywhere!"

"So can I lure you away for a quick coffee break?"

"I can't – I'm flat out here." Sam looked around, and although a few tables were full, many more were not.

"Come on, five minutes won't kill you, I promise if it gets busy, I'll let you get back to it."

"Lily, would you go on, I can hold the fort for a few minutes," Dad said, interrupting me.

"Okay, go sit down then."

I made us two coffees and followed him down to a small table in the corner. I sat down but straight away noticed that the milk jug needed to be refilled. I hopped up to go to the fridge.

"Where are you going now?" Sam asked.

"It needs more milk –" I said, holding up the jug.

"Can't it wait for a few minutes?"

"Sorry – of course it can." I smiled back at him and sat

160

down again. "It's hard to switch off sometimes."

"Guess what?" he said.

"What?"

"I think I have found us the perfect wedding venue."

I felt that familiar knot of anxiety that seemed to be gnawing away at me a lot lately get tighter. My heart started thumping like a small bird inside my chest.

"Where?" I said, hoping that my voice didn't betray me and that I sounded as excited as he was.

"Marita's garden!"

I almost spat out my coffee.

"I know it sounds daft, but it's perfect," he continued.

Marita had an old walled garden where roses and ivy crept along over the old red-brick walls. I had been over there for family parties and barbeques and it was great for entertaining, but for a wedding? Our wedding . . . well, I wasn't so sure . . .

"Her garden is beautiful, we could erect a huge marquee and run fairy lights over the old walls," he continued. "I think it would be magical. Think about it!"

"I guess so –"

"What is it?"

"Nothing."

"You don't want the garden, do you?"

"It's not that –"

"Well, what is it then?"

I looked at his dark eyes where confusion was met with growing impatience. How could I ever find the words to express how I was feeling? I glanced over to see a small queue of three

161

people had started to form. I jumped up. "I better go and help Dad out, but it sounds perfect, Sam." I leaned in and kissed him on the lips.

He looked deflated, the enthusiasm that had been all over his face when he had bounded through the door just minutes earlier had evaporated.

"Lily, I –"

"I'll see you later," I said, quickly cutting him off before he could say anything else to me.

I hurried back over behind the counter and started to serve my hungry customers.

* * *

After I had closed that evening, I stayed in *Baked with Love* longer than usual. I had fallen behind on my paperwork, which I despised doing. It was such a chore. I also needed to finalise my orders before Christmas because a lot of my suppliers would be closing until the New Year. I just wished I could bake all day long and not bother with the other parts involved in running a business.

Frankie called in on her way home from a shoot while I was sweeping the floor.

"I was passing, and I saw the lights were still on. I thought you'd be at home playing with your early Christmas present?" she said with a wink.

"Frankie!" I said, shaking my head as I swept around her.

"So why are you still here? I thought you'd be spending every second that you have with him while he's here." She took off her sunflower yellow bouclé coat and sat down onto a chair.

162

"I've a business to run, I can't let everything slide just because Sam is back – we'll have all Christmas together anyway."

She looked at me quizzically. "Hmmmh."

"What?" I said defensively.

"Well, it's just that you don't seem very happy to have your fiancé home!"

"Of course, I am – it's just –"

"Just what?"

I sighed and pulled out a chair and sat down opposite her. "I don't know . . . he's so keen on the wedding and he wants to set a date, but every time he mentions it, I just feel all panicky inside . . . it's like my whole chest gets tight and I can't breathe. I don't know what is wrong with me, but I didn't feel like this when Marc proposed."

Her eyes widened. "Oh my God, Lily! Are you having doubts about marrying him?"

"No –" I said quickly. "Oh, I don't know, Frankie . . ."

"You don't sound too sure?"

"I've been married before; it's different this time. I'm older now and I know what can go wrong. When I said my vows to Marc, I thought we would be together forever and it only lasted three months! I just want everything to stay the same, things are perfect between us now, and I'm just worried that if I walk down the aisle again, I could be setting myself up for more heartache. Whenever things go right in my life something bad always happens – I'm scared to let anything change."

"So have you told Sam this?"

163

I shook my head. "I can't seem to find the words. How am I supposed to tell him that I love him but I'm having doubts about marrying him? Hell, it sounds ridiculous even to me . . ." I groaned.

"Good luck with that!"

I sighed. "It's a mess – I'm a mess . . ."

"Look, you love him, it's just nerves," she said gently. "After what happened the last time, that's completely normal. You'll be fine in a few weeks once you've had time to get your head around it."

I nodded, willing myself to believe that what she was saying was true, but inside I felt the rising feeling of panic grip hold of me and it wouldn't let go.

CHAPTER 26

It was after nine when I finally put the key in the door to head home. I mounted my bike and cycled over the cobblestones through the dark evening. Christmas lights twinkled magically across the city. Groups of noisy Christmas revellers staggered between bars, starting off the festive celebrations. A couple sat arguing on a bench, the woman's face was red and tear-stained. When I reached our apartment, I let myself in to find Sam sitting at the table eating. It was set for two.

He looked up at me. "I wasn't sure when you were going to be home. I left you a message?"

I fished out my phone from my jacket pocket and had a look. Sure enough, I saw three missed calls from Sam.

"Sorry, I was so engrossed in my order book that I never even looked at it –"

"It doesn't matter. Yours is in the oven." He gestured to the plate of curry he was eating.

"It looks great, thank you, I'm starved."

I continued on to the kitchen and took my dinner from where Sam had left it.

"So, did you think any more about Marita's place?" he asked after I had finished eating.

"Uh-huh," I lied.

"And?"

I plastered a smile on my face. "It sounds great."

"That's it? That's all you have to say about it?"

I placed my cutlery down on the plate.

"Well, yeah," I said, taken aback. "I think it will be lovely."

"Is everything okay between us?" he blurted.

I stopped dead. Fear snaked its way through my body. "Of course, why?"

"It's nothing . . ." He wouldn't meet my eyes.

"What is it, Sam?"

"I just thought you'd show a little bit more interest in our wedding, that's all –"

"Of course, I'm interested."

"Well, I don't know . . . excuse me if I'm wrong, but I thought you might be a bit excited too?"

I felt like a rabbit caught in a trap; there was no way out. I knew I needed to be honest with him. Brutally honest.

"I just don't know what's wrong with me . . ." I blurted.

"You're having doubts about marrying me?" He moved his chair back from the table with a screech. There was no mistaking the hurt in his eyes.

"I'm sorry, Sam. I don't know what it is – I mean, I love you – I know I do, but whenever I think about marrying you . . . well . . . I get all anxious and I'm pretty sure it's not meant to feel like this when you're marrying somebody . . ."

"So it didn't feel like this last time then?" His tone was spiteful, and I knew the comment was barbed.

"I'm sorry, Sam. I'm trying to be honest with you about

166

how I'm feeling. I don't know what is wrong with me –" I started to cry. He stayed rooted to his chair.

"I don't really have anything more I can say to you, Lily. I thought you loved me –"

"I do love you, Sam – that's why I don't understand why I'm feeling like this –"

"Do you know what, Lily, I don't understand it either!"

He got up from the chair and stormed out through the door.

* * *

It was after midnight when Sam returned that night. I lay there listening to the blood ringing in my ears, wondering about where he had gone. When I heard his footsteps in the hallway I waited for him to come into the bedroom, but instead, I heard him settling in for a night on the sofa. I got out of bed after a few minutes and crept into the living room. His jacket was tossed casually over the back of the sofa, and his shoes lay messily on the rug, where he had obviously kicked them off when he came in.

He was already comatose on the sofa. He was still fully clothed and snoring like a trooper. His skin looked silvery under the moonlight. There was a smell of alcohol off his breath. I drew the curtains before taking the throw off the back of the sofa. I placed it over him before returning to bed. I was so worried about what was going to happen to us. All I knew was that I didn't want to lose him, but I was so afraid that I already had.

CHAPTER 27

Sam didn't wake when I got up the next morning. He lay there snoring as I crept out the door to work. The knot of anxiety that had been chasing me around for days had now wound itself so tightly around me that I felt as though I was going to suffocate. It was like I had an elephant sitting on my chest every time I thought about Sam and our future together. Here I was on Christmas Eve and instead of feeling excited about the chance to spend the holidays together, now we had come to an impasse. I knew last night's events had changed everything for us, and I couldn't see a way back from here.

I went to work that day, and Sam didn't call me like he usually would. I didn't feel very merry as customers wished me a happy Christmas, and when I finally turned the sign on the door to Closed to signal the start of the holidays, instead of excited, I just felt deflated. I said goodbye to Dad who had been cheerily wearing a Santa hat. His happy face was in direct contrast to my own worries.

When I reached our block, I chained my bike in the basement and took the lift up to the top floor. Sam was sitting watching TV when I went in.

"Hey there," I said.

He didn't answer me. I made my way over to the sofa and sat down beside him. It was some panel show where they were discussing the best rugby moments of the year.

"How was your day?" I tried again.

He looked at me, his eyes locked on mine, and I could see the pain behind them. I found myself unable to meet them, so I looked down at the floor. He picked up the remote and turned off the TV. Silence fell on the room.

"I think we both want different things, Lily," he said eventually.

"I want you, Sam, I really do, but the wedding . . ."

"I don't get it – if you want to be with me, then you should want to marry me. I have no doubts about you. We've been together for over two years now; we know each other as well as we're ever going to know one another. I can't see where we go from here –"

"Please, Sam, can't we just be as we are now? What we have together is great – we don't need to change that –"

"No, Lily, that's not what I want. I want to be with you for the rest of my life. I want to have children with you."

"And I want that too –"

"Well, then why won't you marry me?"

"I don't know," I said in a small voice. "I was married before, Sam, I'm just not able to even think about doing that again. It brings back too many painful memories – I just can't go there, I'm sorry."

"You see that's exactly the problem here. I've been in denial about it ever since I met you, but I need to face it, you're not over Marc."

"Yes, I am!"

"I think I've always known it, I got you on the rebound, but I had hoped that as time went on that his hold over you would lessen, you know?"

Suddenly, I felt panicked. "I am not in love with Marc, Sam, you have to believe me!"

"But how can I when all your actions tell me otherwise?"

"That's not fair!"

He stood up off the sofa. "I need space, Lily."

I was left reeling. I knew we were in trouble, but I never imagined it was this bad.

"Sam, please – I think that's a step too far. I want to be with you, and yes, I'm not ready for marriage just yet, but I'm sure I will be, I just need time –"

"I'm sorry, I can't do this to myself anymore. It's over." Then he turned and walked away from me.

CHAPTER 28

"What is it? What's going on?" Frankie said as she opened the door to me. She was wearing pyjamas with antlers on the shoulders that looked really uncomfortable for sleeping in, and her thick, wiry hair stood up wildly around her head.

"I didn't know where else to go," I said in a small voice.

She eyed up my tear-stained face and the suitcase by my feet. "It's Christmas Eve! The only person I was expecting tonight was Santa. You'd better come in, what's happened?"

I went through to her living room and plonked myself wearily down on the sofa.

"It's over," I sobbed.

Her eyebrows shot up and her face read shocked. "What do you mean? You and Sam?"

I nodded.

"Jesus, Lily, what the fuck happened?"

"He kept talking about the wedding, he wanted to set a date, but I just came out in a cold sweat every time we spoke about it."

"So you told him you weren't ready then?" she probed gently.

I nodded. "I couldn't hide it from him anymore."

"And he wanted to break up with you? Isn't that a bit unfair?"

"He said I'm not over Marc yet and that he's fed up of living in his shadow. I tried telling him that I've no feelings left for him, but he wouldn't believe me."

"I'm so sorry, Lily. I don't know what to say to you. As shocking as it was when you and Marc broke up, I totally thought you and Sam would be together forever. He loves you! Do you think he has a point about you not being ready to marry him?"

"I love him, Frankie, I really do, but I'm just not ready to rush into another marriage. I tried to make him understand that it's not that I'm not in love with him and I think one day I will be ready to marry him . . ."

"But not now –"

I flopped back against the cushions and exhaled heavily.

"Maybe you need some space to get your head around what it is that you do want?" Frankie suggested.

"I know what I want, Frankie! I want him!" I wailed.

"Then you need to tell him that!"

"I have but he won't listen. He has such a hang-up about Marc; he thinks he got me on the rebound."

"He has a point –"

I sat up straight. "Sam is worth ten of Marc."

"He is, so what's the problem then?" Frankie said evenly.

I lowered my voice to whisper. "I can't build myself up for all of that again; the excitement, the hopes and dreams, and then if something went wrong . . . To have the whole fuss and for what? To be left red-faced three months later because your new husband does a runner with an actress? I couldn't go through all

174

of that again. Even just thinking about it makes me sweat. I don't see why we can't just stay as we are? We're going along just fine – we're in love – why do we have to jeopardise what we have?"

"It doesn't always have to go wrong, Lily," she said softly. "What happened with Marc was very bad luck."

"This is me we're talking about here – if it can go wrong, it will go wrong."

"Oh, Lily," she sighed, pulling me into a hug. "I'm so sorry."

CHAPTER 29

That night Frankie tucked me up in the bedroom with the wildly clashing pink and orange walls once again. I hated this room and all that it represented. It was the same bed I had stayed in after I had walked in on Marc with Nadia. I couldn't believe I was back here again, except this time I was worse off because I didn't even have my home in Ballyrobin to go back to. There were tenants in it now. I texted Sam to say that I loved him no matter what he thought, and I kept checking my phone for the rest of the night to see if he had replied to me, but there was nothing back from him. He wasn't one for petty squabbles or holding grudges, so I knew that this was it, he was done with me.

I was already awake when I saw the morning light creeping around the edges of the blind the next morning. It was Christmas Day, my favourite day of the year, but I couldn't feel any less in the mood for Christmas if I tried. Tears came into my eyes. This wasn't how it was supposed to be this year; when Sam had surprised me by coming home, I had imagined us spending Christmas morning snuggling in bed together, exchanging gifts, and maybe even returning to bed afterwards. I had visions of lazy days of lounging around together, stuffing our faces with food and trying to burn it off with long walks in the chilly December air. I had pictured steaming mugs of hot chocolate, tender kisses under the mistletoe, and catching up with everyone at Sam's parents' annual Christmas night bash. It was supposed to be romantic and beautiful and not end up with me staying in Frankie's room of heartbreak.

I reached for my phone to check in case he had had a change of heart and had called me, but there was nothing. I dialled his number again, but he didn't pick up. Instead, I heard his voicemail greeting in that gorgeous husky tone. I physically ached to wake up beside him where he would take me into his arms and I would lay my head against the solidness of his chest.

I climbed out of bed eventually and dragged myself into the shower.

"Happy Christmas," Frankie said when I made an appearance in the kitchen.

I grunted.

"How are you doing?"

"I've been better."

"Do you want a fry?" she asked as she took sausages and bacon out of the fridge.

"I couldn't stomach food right now." I felt sick as I thought back over the day before. The hurt on Sam's face would stay with me forever. I pulled out a chair and sat down at the table. "I just can't believe this has happened!" I was still reeling from the shock at how my whole world had come crashing down around me in the last twenty-four hours. "I mean, it's not like I have any feelings left for Marc!" I sighed and slumped down in the seat.

"I know that, but does Sam? Look, he might have calmed down since last night, so why don't you call him now? Tell him that you love him but you just need time, he'll understand –"

"He's not answering my calls – I really think this is it for us."

"I'm sorry, Lily, I really am."

When I had finally summoned up the courage, I called Dad to ask him to tell Clara that Sam and I wouldn't be joining them for Christmas dinner like we had planned. I couldn't face calling her myself. Plus, I didn't want to sit across the table from her and watch her play happy families with Tom even though she was plotting and scheming behind his back about how to take him to the cleaners. I think that might have sent me over the edge completely.

"What's wrong with you, Lily?" Dad asked when I told him we wouldn't be going over.

"Sam and I broke up."

I heard something drop in the background with a clatter. "Ah, Lily, what happened?"

"He thinks that because I'm not ready to marry him that I'm not over Marc."

"And do you think he has a point?"

"No, Dad, I love him, I know I do . . . I'm just scared about marriage."

"Well, did you tell him that?"

"He just doesn't get it."

"Give him time, Lily, he'll come round."

"I don't think he will." I broke down then and began to sob.

"It'll all work out, Lily, these things always do. If it's meant to be, it's meant to be."

I sat on the chair with tears spilling down my face. I couldn't be without Sam, I just couldn't.

CHAPTER 30

It had been a horrible Christmas. I spent the day itself alone in Frankie's place. She had tried to persuade me to join her family, and Dad tried his best to coax me into going to Clara's with him even just for an hour, but I couldn't face it. I couldn't face anyone. I had tried repeatedly to get in touch with Sam, but he still wouldn't return my calls or messages.

Every time I thought about him my heart ached. Why did it have to be so hard? Why could I never seem to find true love the way you saw it in the movies or the way my mum and dad were? Maybe I was an old-fashioned romantic, maybe it just didn't happen that way anymore these days.

Even though he had asked me not to contact him, I had called over to his apartment anyway hoping that the space of being apart for a few days over Christmas would have given him time to calm down. I hoped that he might be willing to talk to me at least but he had been out at the time. In the end, I had left him a note telling him that I loved him and that I didn't want him to go back to New York on these terms. I knew that once he was on the other side of the Atlantic it would be impossible to get things back on track between us again. I asked if he would meet me just to talk before he went back, but he never called. I was distraught at the thought of him flying back there without having had the chance to talk face-to-face first.

The days went past until it was finally time to re-open *Baked with Love* after the Christmas break. I was never so glad to see the back of Christmas. When the day had broken, I decided to head in early. I knew that moping around, feeling sorry for myself was not going to help me. There were myriad things I could be doing there to get myself back open and hopefully take my mind off the mess that was my love life.

I put my key in the lock and pushed the door. Even the sound of my little bell failed to put a smile on my face like it usually would. The Christmas decorations, so colourful and jubilant in the days before Christmas, now seemed to be mocking me. When I had last been in here, I had had excitement fizzing inside my tummy at the thoughts of cosying up with Sam over the holidays. Even though it wasn't yet the New Year, I started to pull them all down. I just wanted Christmas to be over.

By the time Dad came in, I was already way ahead of where I would usually be.

"You've been busy," he said, gesturing to the walls that now seemed so stark and bare and somehow even more depressing than before.

"The sooner the silly season is over the better."

"Now come on, Lily, don't be a misery guts – you love Christmas. I'll make us a cuppa, you go sit down." Dad put a pot of tea down on the table followed by a generous slice of carrot cake. "Get that into you," he said, sliding the plate towards me.

"I can't, Dad." The smell of the nutmeg made me want to gag. My stomach just wasn't able for food. The only upside to this heartache was that my appetite had well and truly vanished.

182

"Did you get to talk to Sam before he went back?"

I shook my head. "He left yesterday."

"Lily, I'm so sorry," Dad said. "Give him time, maybe a little bit of headspace will help him to come round."

I nodded, not trusting myself to speak. The truth was I had already given him space, I didn't see how anymore could help.

At nine o'clock we both hooked our aprons over our necks and got ready to welcome the day's customers. It was a painfully quiet day. The streets beyond the bottle glass windows were empty. Most of the nearby offices wouldn't be reopening until January. As the day went on, a few lonely souls trickled through the door; I guessed these were the ones who had drawn the short straw and been picked to work over Christmas. Most other people were at home spending time with loved ones, which is what you should be doing over Christmas, I thought sadly.

After lunch, the bell tinkled and I saw Clara come in with the boys.

"Lily, Dad!" she said brightly. I noticed she had had her hair done and was immaculately dressed in a silk blouse tucked into skinny leg trousers. She didn't look like a woman nursing a broken heart. "God this place is empty," she said, looking around her and shaking her head.

"Well, a lot of people are still off work –" I said a touch defensively.

"So did you and Sam sort things out?" she asked when the boys were seated on the sofa with hot chocolates. Dad had told her everything that had happened on Christmas day.

I shook my head. "He's already back in New York."

183

"All men are bastards, sheer and utter bastards!" she hissed. Cursing was so uncharacteristic for her that I almost laughed. I didn't want to upset her by telling her that Sam wasn't a bastard, in fact he was a really good guy; we just had a difference that neither of us seemed able to bridge.

"Us McDermott ladies will stick together," she continued. "Tom and Sam will be sorry when we're finished with them!" She wagged her finger.

I saw Dad raise his eyebrows at her. "So, what are you doing here?" he asked.

"Oh, just taking a little detour from a reconnaissance mission."

"You were following him?" he said aghast.

"Of course, Dad. I can't be naïve about this. I need to build up a case. I didn't spend years studying to be a lawyer for nothing – I knew my training would come in handy one day."

"So where is he gone?" I asked.

"Well, he said he was going into the office for a couple of hours."

"And?" I said wide-eyed to see what she had found.

"Well, he's in the office . . . but I know it's a ruse."

"Was there anyone else with him?" If he was having an affair with a work colleague, the quiet office during the Christmas break might be the perfect meeting place.

She shook her head. "His was the only car in the car park, but who's to say she didn't come on foot?"

"Or who's to say that he isn't actually doing work?" Dad said, playing devil's advocate. None of this sat easy with him.

We both still found it hard to believe that Tom was conducting an affair, but Clara had found the underwear in her bed after all and they didn't get there innocently.

"Whose side are you on?" she asked, looking at both of us through narrowed eyes.

"We're on your side of course," Dad cajoled, "but I still think you need to give the man a fair hearing. There might be a perfectly good explanation for all of this."

"Dad, please, if you're going to suggest I'm confusing the knickers with part of the Christmas garlands again then don't –"

Dad started to blush at Clara's use of the word knickers.

"My colour scheme is white and silver this year anyway," she continued.

"So did you find any more proof yet?" I said. The last time I had spoken to her she had found the offshore bank account, but she had been digging so much, who knew what else she had uncovered.

"Well, no . . . but do you know what he got me for Christmas?"

"What?"

"A gym membership!"

"And what's wrong with that?" Dad asked.

"He's trying to tell me to lose weight – the cheeky bastard! He could do with losing a few pounds himself!"

For a woman hitting forty, Clara was in excellent shape and Tom was always complimenting her on her figure, so I really doubted he meant anything sinister by it. Suddenly, I found myself feeling sorry for Tom. "He probably didn't mean you to take offence to it; he knows you like taking care of yourself."

"Ha!" she spat. "Oh yes, I'm taking care of myself all right," she said with a wild glint in her eyes.

"But have you noticed him sneaking off anywhere over the break to meet her?" I said.

She shook her head. "It's the Christmas holidays, so he knows I would ask questions if he said he was going somewhere. He is being extra careful. He's clever but he will slip up, and when the bastard does, I'll be there to catch him out."

Suddenly I felt exhausted, Clara was so conniving and scheming that I found it wearisome. Instead of feeling galvanised by our similar experiences, I just felt worn out. How did she have the energy to play games with him? Why didn't she just talk to him like a normal person?

"I don't know, Clara, I don't have a good feeling about all of this cloak-and-dagger stuff," Dad warned.

"Just because I'm not a pushover like you two – honestly, I do wonder sometimes how we are related."

"Just be careful," he continued.

She swung around in a huff and shouted down to the boys, "Come on, Jacob and Joshua, it's time to go now."

CHAPTER 31

January arrived in an unforgiving blast of cold. I had rung in the New Year on my own. Frankie had tried to drag me out with her but I couldn't face it, so I had taken a plate of all my favourite cakes (Heavenly Orange slathered in cream cheese icing, lemon curd tart made with the butteriest shortcrust pastry, and my Baileys white chocolate cake) and a big mug of tea to bed with me. But when I took a bite, I couldn't enjoy them, I felt queasy and miserable. There was no joy in my life without Sam. I used to love New Year's Eve, full of hope and optimism for all that lay ahead. Out with the old and in with the new and all that. That's why I had chosen it as the day I married Marc. This year would have been our third wedding anniversary and I despised the day ever since.

Over the next few weeks I went through the motions, and somehow I got through each day. I would plaster a smile on my face as I beat my batter and served my customers, but inside my heart was torn into tiny pieces. I ached for Sam. I couldn't sleep or eat. I felt physically sick constantly. I had tried calling and texting him several times since he had returned to New York, but he never replied. The mornings were the worst; my body longed to feel his strong arms around me as I woke. It was as if I was waking from a nightmare over and over again, except it was worse because this was my reality.

One day I was working my way through the queue when I heard a familiar voice say, "Double espresso, please."

I raised my head and felt my stomach lurch when I saw it was Marc standing there.

"Hi, Lily," he said with a wide smile spreading across his face. Before I knew what was happening, he leant forward and kissed me. I pulled back quickly and felt heat make its way up along my face. We were standing in the middle of my café in broad daylight; I was embarrassed in front of the customers.

"What are you doing here?" I stammered. It had been two years since I had last seen him, and the sight of him had caught me off guard.

"Is that any way to talk to your husband?"

"Ex-husband," I said through gritted teeth. Marc was the very last person I wanted to see here.

"Now, now, I just want to talk to you. I haven't seen you in ages –"

"Well, I'm busy."

I saw Dad, who had been clearing off a table, looking over at us with narrowed eyes.

"Are you okay, Lily?" he asked, coming over.

"Mr McD! The apron suits you," Marc said, laughing.

"Hi, Marc," Dad said icily.

"I'm sure you can spare five minutes for me, Lily. Come on, for old times' sake."

I noticed some of the customers looking funnily at me as they recognised Marc's face from the gossip magazines and they tried to work out what was going on.

188

"Go and sit down, I'll bring your espresso over in a minute," I hissed.

"Oh, could you get me one of those lemon muffins – they look great – actually, do you have any without gluten? I'm going gluten free these days."

I felt the rage course through my body.

"So what do you want?" I asked, setting the mug and plate with a gluten-free coconut cream cake down on the table a few minutes later and taking the seat opposite him.

"This place is really good actually, Lily," he said, looking around. "I can't believe you own it –"

"You sound surprised –"

"Well, yeah, I am – it's like . . . a proper bakery. Somewhere I would actually go, y'know?"

"Yes, Marc, it is a 'proper' bakery. What did you think it was going to be? It's a lot of hard work, I won't lie, but I'm very proud of it. I love coming to work every day."

"So, how's it all going with the new guy?" He bit into the cake.

"His name is Sam, and it's been over two years now, so he's not new –"

"Yeah, Sam," he said through a mouthful of chewed food.

"We broke up –"

"Sorry to hear that."

"No, you're not, you're just glad to know somebody else who is just as much of a fuck-up as you."

"Would I be a bad person if I said you're kind of right?" He smiled wryly at me.

189

I shook my head. "So how are little Marley and Nadia?"

"Marley is great; she's a pain. I don't know what I ever saw in her."

"Well, you must have seen something if you were able to walk out on your marriage after three months!"

"Touché!" He picked up a sugar sachet and flicked it back and forth between his fingers. "We're trying to make a go of it, but if we didn't have Marley I think we would have broken up a long time ago to be honest . . ."

I had heard all this before from Marc. He was the master of playing the sympathy card, but I wasn't going to get sucked into feeling sorry for him. I had wised up to his antics.

"So what has you here?" I asked, wanting him to get to the point.

"I want to sell the house."

"You want to sell Ballyrobin?"

He nodded.

"We can't sell it, Marc, it's still in negative equity."

"But I need the money –"

"Well, if we sold it tomorrow, we wouldn't get any – in fact, we'd owe the bank money."

"Really?"

How stupid was he? I was in disbelief that this would come as news to him. "Well yeah, have you even looked at the property prices in that estate lately?"

"No."

"Well, maybe you should!"

He was so clueless; he couldn't even do the basic research

to see if it made financial sense to sell it. He lived in his own self-centred bubble.

"Look, Marc, it's not really any of my business, but Nadia is one of Ireland's best-known actresses, surely you couldn't be that hard up?"

"Well, we've broken up actually, so she keeps telling me to get a job, but it's hard to get decent acting roles, especially in Ireland. The real work is in LA, but it's not like I can go there now that we have a baby."

I had to stifle back a laugh. He was deluded. As if having a baby was the sole reason why he couldn't land a prime Hollywood role.

"Well, maybe there are other jobs you could do while you do auditions?"

"Like what?"

"I don't know, an office job or work in a shop or something?"

He looked aghast. "I couldn't do that!"

"Well, then don't come complaining to me that you're broke!" He was pathetic. I almost felt sorry for him. It was hard to believe that I had spent such a long part of my life with him and had been devastated by our break-up, whereas now I couldn't help but wonder how I had put up with him for so long.

I looked up towards the counter and saw a small queue was beginning to form. Dad looked under pressure. "Look, I have to go, the lunchtime rush has started."

"Oh . . . right."

I stood up to leave, but he made no move to go.

191

"Do you think I could get a refill?" He signalled to his now empty mug.

I felt my blood boil. I shoved back my chair with a screech and stood up. As I made my way back to the counter, my legs felt wobbly. I tried to walk but they wouldn't work properly. Suddenly, I felt a loud ringing in my ears as if I was being chased by a swarm of angry bees. The counter started to shimmer in front of me.

"Lily, Lily, are you okay?" I could hear Dad asking me somewhere on the periphery, but I wasn't able to answer him. It sounded as though he was miles away.

Suddenly, the ground seemed to melt away before me and I was falling to the floor.

CHAPTER 32

Ow, ow, ow . . . my head was throbbing; it felt as though my brain was pulsing against my skull. I could hear voices talking in hushed tones around me.

"Lily?" I heard a voice from the periphery ask. "Are you awake?"

I wanted whomever it was to just leave me alone. I was so tired, and my head was thumping.

"What happened to her?" Another voice asked.

"I don't know; Marc showed up at the café. One minute they were talking, and God knows what he must have said to her because the next thing I see she is collapsed on the floor and is out cold."

I recognised the voices, but I didn't know where I was or why they were talking about me.

"Lily, can you hear me?" The voice was insistent.

I slowly began to peel my eyes open. Light rushed in and it hurt, so I closed them down again.

"She's awake! She just opened her eyes!"

I tried once more and this time I let them adjust to the room around me. The first person I saw was Clara. I shifted my eyes and saw Dad was beside her.

"Oh thank God, you're awake," he said, squeezing my hand.

"Where am I?" was all I could manage to get out.

"You're in the hospital, love. You fainted in the café. You had a bad fall and were out cold. You gave us all a fright." He was smiling kindly at me. "How are you feeling?"

I tried to nod but my head was so sore when I tried to move it.

"Don't stir now, you've a lot of bruising, easy does it."

"What happened?" My voice came out as a croak.

"Well, I don't know . . . Marc came in –" Dad said.

"Marc?" I grimaced.

Dad nodded. "You two were talking . . . I don't know what happened. I was busy making a coffee for a customer and the next thing I heard a commotion, and when I turned around to see what was going on, you were on the floor! Some of the customers who saw what happened said you hit your head off a table on the way down. The doctors are running some tests to make sure everything is okay with you."

"It's probably just low blood pressure." Clara was shaking her head knowingly. "It happens to me all the time."

"Clara's right, I'm sure it's nothing to worry about." Dad smiled weakly.

I tried to recall what had led to me being here, but my mind was blank. I had no recollection of anything that had happened earlier that day, especially of talking to Marc.

Suddenly, the curtain was being pulled back and a man in a white coat came in clutching a file against his chest. "Ah Lily, I'm glad to see you're awake. I'm Doctor Marshall. How are you feeling?"

194

"A bit sore."

"You had a nasty concussion. It'll take a while before you start feeling like yourself again. Can I ask how have you been feeling lately? Have you had any episodes before? Any dizziness or blackouts?"

I shook my head. "I've been fine. It's the first time anything like this has ever happened to me."

He nodded. "So we've run some bloods, and we've just got the results back from the lab. I think we know why it happened – "

"What is it?" I asked, suddenly concerned that there was a reason for this and it wasn't just "one of those things."

I noticed he shifted feet and cleared his throat. "Well, perhaps your family could leave us alone together for a few minutes –"

Suddenly, I was scared. Was he going to tell me I was dying? Was this the bit where they told me I had six weeks to live so I needed to start ticking off my bucket list before I kicked the bucket myself?

"No, I want them to stay with me," I said quickly. I needed their support for whatever he was going to tell me. I know I'm such a catastrophist, but I can't help it.

He pulled out a chair and sat down. "Very well then, Lily, I don't know if you realise it, but you're actually pregnant." His face was beaming down on me as if it was the best news ever.

Pregnant? The words seemed so out of context. It was as if he was speaking a different vocabulary to me, it didn't make any sense.

195

"Pregnant? But I can't be –"

"Well, your bloods would suggest differently –"

"But I – I'm sure I'm not – I'm single –"

"Look, it's none of my business how the . . ." he cleared his throat, "event . . . came about, but the fact of the matter is that you're pregnant. I'm sorry if this has come as a shock to you or if your circumstances aren't ideal. I can ask one of the hospital counsellors to have a word with you if you would like?"

I risked a glance at Clara who was holding her head in her hands and shaking it, saying, "I don't believe it," over and over again.

"Often the change in hormone levels associated with early pregnancy can cause a drop in blood pressure resulting in dizziness and or fainting. Going by your HCG levels, I would estimate that you are about eight weeks along, although we would need to do a dating scan to confirm that."

"I see . . ." I said, reeling with the shock.

"So who's the Dad, Lily?" Clara hissed at me as soon as Doctor Marshall had left us alone again. "You must have known him for a sum total of weeks. Unless you're the second coming of the Virgin Mary? Well done, little sister, once again you have made a complete and utter cock-up of your life!"

"Ah, Lily, it's not Marc's, is it?" Dad asked, the blood suddenly draining from his face.

"No, Dad, of course it's not!" I said affronted. "It can only be Sam's – I haven't been with anyone else –"

"Well, putting on the pity act isn't going to get you out of this one!"

196

"Now, now, Clara," Dad intervened.

"But they're not even together anymore! She's going to be another single mother scrounging off the state. I cannot believe you allowed this to happen, Lily. Didn't you ever hear of contraception?"

"I – I – I did – we did –"

"Well, clearly it wasn't very effective!"

"It's not the end of the world. Plenty of people do it alone these days, times have changed," Dad said.

"Oh, quit your neo-liberal antics, Dad, for Christ's sake!" Clara said. "It's a disaster!"

I closed my eyes. My head was throbbing, and the news I had just learnt had made it a million times worse. Clara was not helping. I just wanted to get rid of her.

"Don't you realise the magnitude of this, Lily?" she continued. "Do you know how demanding being a parent is? You can't even support yourself, let alone a baby! And you want to do it on your own?" She scoffed. "You've ruined your whole life."

"Clara, Lily has had a tough day, she's exhausted, she needs to rest now," Dad said to her. He turned back to me. "Are you sure you're okay, love? I know this is a big shock, but we're here for you, you know that, don't you? No matter what happens you won't be doing this on your own."

I briefly opened my eyes and nodded at him before closing then again and pretending to fall back asleep. After a few moments, I heard them packing up to go with Clara muttering, "just when I thought she was finally getting her life together . . ."

197

After they had left, I felt the weight of tears pressing behind my eyes. They spilled over and down along my face until the pillowcase underneath me grew damp. I couldn't believe what I had been told. How had I not realised it? Now that I thought about it, I couldn't remember when I had last had my period. I had been so upset by everything with Sam and then busy with *Baked with Love* that I just hadn't noticed. It explained why I had been feeling so nauseous; I had been putting it down to heartache and missing Sam. What was I going to do now? Sam was gone, and I was alone. The timing couldn't have been worse, especially as I was trying to get *Baked with Love* off the ground, how would I do that and mind a baby? I couldn't have a baby. I just couldn't. I could barely look after myself.

CHAPTER 33

The next morning I woke to the sound of the breakfast trolley being pushed into the ward. Spoons rattled against teacups and plates shuddered against each other as it came closer to me. The curtain was pulled back and a tray was placed on the table at the end of the bed. I could smell mushrooms and it made me want to heave.

I placed my hands on the skin of my stomach and tried to imagine what was going on in there. It was hard to believe that right now there was a baby, or probably a tadpole at this stage, growing away without any input from me, and yet I had been completely unaware of the whole thing. I couldn't believe that I was already two months along. Didn't people begin showing at around three months? I felt so unprepared for it all, both emotionally and financially. If I had still been with Sam, although it would have been a shock, I know we would have worked it out together. He would have been supportive during something like this. He would have calmly allayed all my fears and told me that everything was going to be all right, but now that we were no longer together, I didn't even have that comfort.

I heard the trolley being wheeled back in a while afterwards, and the catering assistant shook her head in dismay as she lifted my untouched breakfast tray back onto her trolley again.

A while later a head peeped around the side of the curtain. "Lily?"

"Frankie!"

She hurried over to my bedside and hugged me. "Thank God, you're okay. You gave me such a fright when you didn't come home, and then you weren't answering your phone. I was going up the walls, but then your Dad called me late last night and told me what happened."

"Did he tell you everything?"

"Well yeah, I think so . . ." She sat down onto the chair beside my bed. "What do you mean everything?

"Well, the reason I collapsed –"

"There's a reason?"

I nodded. "I'm pregnant, Frankie –"

She gasped. "You're what?"

"Pregnant."

"I heard you, but how?"

"Your guess is as good as mine." I threw my head back against the pillow. "They reckon I'm about eight weeks along. It must have happened in New York."

"So it's Sam's then?"

"Of course, it is, sure I haven't even looked at another man since our break-up."

"Have you told him yet?"

I shook my head. "I need to get my own head around it first . . . it's such a mess."

She reached out for my hand and spoke softly. "Do you think you'll keep it?"

200

I nodded. "I think so," I said in a small voice. Even though circumstances were far from ideal, I couldn't see me ever going through with an abortion.

"Look, you're hardly a teenager, there are worse situations out there. I know you and Sam are no longer together, but it doesn't mean he still can't be a part of this baby's life. And you have your Dad and me. And Clara –" She had a wry smile on her face.

"I know, but it's just not the way I imagined things turning out . . . Whenever I think about starting a family, I picture me and the baby's dad together. I imagine us going to all the appointments, shopping for buggies, him holding my hand in the labour ward while I curse for Ireland! I want all of that – I don't want to do it like this . . ." The tears started up again.

"Hey, don't get too far ahead of yourself, let's take one day at a time," Frankie soothed. "First things first though, you need to tell Sam –"

I nodded. "I know."

"Call him, he might surprise you."

"I doubt it."

We were interrupted by the curtain being pulled back. "Visiting hours aren't until six o'clock, what are you doing here?" a stern nurse said to Frankie. "It's important that our patients get their rest."

"I'm sorry, I'm going now," she said contritely. She bent over and planted a kiss on my forehead. "Try and get some sleep. And remember, call Sam."

* * *

I was discharged from hospital the following morning. They told me to start taking folic acid and to book in with my GP for my antenatal care. Dad was holding the fort in *Baked with Love*, so Frankie collected me from the hospital.

"So did you tell Sam yet?" she said when we were stopped at a red light.

"Not yet," I said, looking out the window.

"Well, shouldn't you tell him sooner rather than later?"

"I guess . . ."

"Lily, you need to tell him –"

"I will!" My tone was impatient. I wished she would stop pestering me about it.

We fell silent as we drove through the Dublin traffic. Frankie turned right onto the quays heading towards her apartment.

"Actually, Frankie, can you drop me off at work?"

She looked at me incredulously. "Please say you're joking?"

"What?"

"No way, Lily! You heard what the doctor said – you have to take it easy for the rest of the week!"

"I just want to see that the place is okay – I promise I'll only stay for a few minutes."

She raised her eyebrows.

"What?" I said.

"Your Dad is well able to manage. I know you, once you get your foot in the door, I won't be able get you out of there again. *Baked with Love* is fine, you on the other hand need to rest!"

When we got home, I was wiped out. I wasn't sure if it was the concussion or a pregnancy symptom or the shock of discovering that I was pregnant or maybe it was a combination of all three.

Frankie placed a blanket over me as I sat on the sofa with my legs curled up underneath me watching a repeat of A Place in the Sun. She handed me a cup of tea and a slice of dry toast. It was all I could stomach. I was still feeling quite nauseous, but at least now I had a reason for it.

"It's morning time in New York, why don't you give him a ring now?" she said after a while.

"Could you just leave it please, Frankie?" I snapped, pulling my blanket tightly around me.

"All right then!" she said, getting huffy back with me. "But you can't put it off forever."

CHAPTER 34

The next morning I listened from bed as Frankie got ready for work, and as soon as I heard the slam of the door, I got out after her and headed straight into the shower. When I was finished, I suddenly felt a wave of nausea assail me. I reached the toilet just in time to spill my guts into the bowl. Beads of sweat broke out across my forehead as I sat on the cool tiles afterwards. It was like my body was suddenly waking up to the fact that it was pregnant and was now going into full-on symptom mode. When I started to feel a bit better, I dressed and headed for my bakery.

"Lily, what the hell are you doing here?" Dad said as soon as I came in through the door.

"I'm going to work, what does it look like?" I said, walking past him and hanging my apron over my neck.

"But I thought you were told to rest –"

"I feel fine and there's no point in me sitting around in Frankie's place all day, I only end up feeling worse about everything."

"But you can't go against what the doctor said, Lily, that's just madness!"

"I'm pregnant not incapacitated! Anyway, I'm better off in here, keeping busy. It helps take my mind off everything."

"Well, if you say so . . ." He was reluctant.

"I'm telling you, Dad, I'm fine."

"Well, take it easy, no heavy lifting, do you hear me? And if you feel in any way funny, you sit down straight away, okay?"

"Yes, Dad, now stop fussing," I said, groaning.

I saw Dad had loaded the ovens with scones which was one job taken care of so I decided that now would be a good time to try out my new cronut recipe. I had been dying to give it a whirl since I came home from New York. It was a complex, time-consuming recipe with lots of steps that had to be done properly or the pastry wouldn't come out right, but I needed something challenging to take my mind off the mess that was my life. I mixed the yeast, milk, butter, salt, and flour together until the dough came together. Then after I had chilled it, I began the lamination process. I rolled the pastry out and generously slathered butter all over it. I was so engrossed in the sequence of folding, chilling, and turning the pastry to perfect the lamination that suddenly I seemed to forget about my worries. Baking really was therapy for the soul.

I came home that evening and I flung my bag down on Frankie's sofa. She had called to tell me that she was going along to some wrap party so she wouldn't be home. I had lied to her and told her that I had stayed in bed all day. To be honest, I was relieved that she was going to be late home. She had been continuously hounding me about telling Sam, so I was glad to avoid her for one night. I walked over, pulled back the glass door leading out to the balcony, and went outside into the cool night air. I breathed deeply into my lungs. I didn't feel good. I was weary from the day and the stress of worrying about how I was going to tell Sam. I rested my elbows on the railing and looked at the city lights, stretching out for miles before me. I was sick of adulting. I was sick of trying to hold everything together by a string only to have it all fall apart anyway. I wanted to fly away to a desert island where no stress or demands could find me. Or a nunnery would work too. One of those enclosed orders where you lived amongst other nuns and you had to take a vow of silence. My whole life was a disaster. A big, huge disaster and I didn't know where to turn. The tears started to spill down my face. I was going to be doing this on my own, and I was so scared.

CHAPTER 35

Baked with Love was busy the next morning, there always seemed to be a queue. Don't get me wrong, I wasn't complaining but it was so unexpected. It was usually just myself and Dad looking at each other for hours on end, but today we were kept on our toes. My cronuts, which I had added onto the chalkboard menu that morning, were proving to be a big draw. I had hovered over them after I removed them from the fryer, waiting for them to cool on the wire rack. As soon as I could taste them without the risk of burning myself, I had lifted one up and bit down into the sugary dough, sending a shower of thick flakes cascading onto my lap. I was met with the nicest surprise on the inside: the pastry was lighter than air – it literally melted in my mouth. Then came the pièce de résistance when the tip of my tongue exploded as the flavour of the rosewater ganache filling hit my taste buds. I had barely swallowed it when suddenly my stomach began turning in that familiar way that I had so quickly grown used to and I had to run to the bathroom just in time to throw up into the bowl. When I was finished, I sat up and wiped the beads of sweat from my brow. I wanted to cry; I had been looking forward to sampling them all morning. This damn morning sickness was killing me. I would open the fridge and the smell would make me heave. Or I suddenly seemed to have an aversion to the smell of nutmeg and couldn't stand to use it my recipes. How was I meant to get through the day working with food if I was like this?

"There's a delivery here for you to sign," Dad said to me just as I was coming out of the bathroom. "Sick again?" he asked when he saw my ghostlike face.

I nodded. "This is hell."

"You'll start feeling better in a few weeks, wait and see."

I went back out to the front and the man presented me with a docket to sign. I took it from him and had just begun signing for it when he said, "Lily – it is you?"

I looked up at his face, it was familiar, but I couldn't place it. Then suddenly it clicked. "Oh my God, Piotr!"

Piotr was the homeless man who used to sit begging outside the supermarket in Ballyrobin. He was originally a Polish migrant who had come to Ireland to work in the building trade during the Celtic Tiger, but when the property market crashed, he had been scattered amongst the debris of the fallout. I used to buy him a hot drink or sandwich whenever I saw him, but now that I had left Ballyrobin, I didn't see him anymore. I had often wondered what way his life had turned out, but judging by his appearance today, things had worked out pretty well for him.

"How've you been? You look great!" I gushed.

"I got job, Lily. Now I have house. I have girlfriend –"

"I'm so happy for you!"

He looked at the delivery label and saw the package was addressed to me. "This is your café?"

I nodded. "It sure is."

"I think we both have success," Piotr said, grinning at me. "I am happy I see you, I want to say thank you, you were always so kind to me. When you sit on the street nobody looks at you, but you talked to me and I say thank you."

I began to blush. "Will you stay and have a coffee?"

"No, I go now, I have twenty-six more deliveries today and my girlfriend, Ana, no like me late home."

"Well, it's been so lovely to see you."

After he had left, I couldn't help but feel a little cheered up. I was so pleased that his life had worked out okay. It put my own problems into perspective, no matter what happened I had a roof over my head and a job that I loved. There were people facing far greater battles than I ever would.

I got back to work and was shocked when all my cronuts had sold out before lunchtime. I thought I had had enough to last the day and even then have some left over for Father Joe. I would need to put them on the menu more often if they were going to be this much of a success.

We were just taking a breather after a mental lunchtime when two young girls came in the door. One was wearing black leggings and an army green bomber jacket over it. The other wore a crop top over jeans. They flicked their hair back and forth, then the girl in the crop top pouted while her friend held up her phone and took a photo of her. Then they switched over. Then they both leaned in and got a selfie together. I looked at them in amusement, and eventually they ordered two lattes. No food. They sat down on the sofa with their heads buried in their phones not talking to each other.

211

I didn't think much of it until we had a group of teenage girls come in later. They were still in their school uniforms, but their faces were immaculately made up with sculpted eyebrows and contoured cheekbones and they all had long manes of carefully styled hair. I thought it was odd because we never had teenagers in unless they were with their parents. At first I presumed they had heard about the cronuts and wanted to taste the new craze, but when they didn't even ask for them and instead just ordered coffees, I was confused.

That night I came in the door from *Baked with Love* in an exhausted and sticky mess. I wearily flopped down onto Frankie's sofa.

"How was your day?" she asked when she came home later. She had been angry when I had confessed that I had returned to work, but she knew that she was wasting her breath by continuing to bang on about it.

"Busy, for once. I made cronuts and they all sold out before lunch!"

"You see? Word of mouth is catching on! So, did you call Sam yet?"

I shook my head. Frankie was like a broken record. Every time she saw me she asked the same thing.

"No time like the present." She handed me the phone.

I passed it back to her. "Just leave it, Frankie."

"You can't put it off forever, Lily."

I ignored her and continued to stare at the TV screen.

"Here I got you this," she said in a softer voice as she handed me a paper bag.

212

I took it from her and looked inside and saw there was a book. I lifted it out and looked at the cover. It was a week-by-week guide to pregnancy.

"Oh my God . . ." I said. "Thanks, Frankie . . . " I was shocked. Even though she kept hassling me about telling Sam, she really was being so supportive. Suddenly I felt a swell of gratitude for my friend. "I'm sorry for being such a moody cow lately."

"Hey, you can't help it, it's your hormones – you're producing more oestrogen and progesterone now – I've already read up on it for you."

I couldn't help but crack a smile.

"You're going to be a great mum, Lily," she said softly.

This set me off, and soon fat tears coursed down my cheeks.

"Oh, Frankie," I cried, "I don't want to do this alone."

"You're not doing this alone, you have me, remember?"

I nodded. "But I can't believe I will be somebody's mother. I don't feel responsible enough to mind another person."

She handed me a tissue, and I wiped my eyes and blew my nose.

"You'll get there, wait and see, once you hold that baby in your arms I bet you any money that those mothering instincts will just kick in." She reached over and squeezed my hand.

"How do you know?"

"Well, I read up on it . . ."

Even though I felt utterly miserable, I couldn't help but laugh at her enthusiasm.

"I'm exhausted, I think I'm going to have an early night," I said after a while.

"Well, you are growing an entire other person, it's bound to knacker you."

"I want to say thanks, Frankie. You literally have been amazing. I couldn't do this without you."

She began to blush and she wouldn't meet my eye. "I think the hormones are making you soppy now."

I went into the bedroom and changed into my pyjamas. As I looked at my reflection in the mirror, my stomach was so bloated. Although never in my life had I a flat stomach, it was definitely a lot bigger than usual. I ran my hands over it and it was rock hard. My breasts were swollen too. I was sure people were going to start thinking that I was eating all the cakes I made in *Baked with Love*.

I collapsed in a heap on the bed. My feet were throbbing from running around all day, and my head was pounding with stress. I lifted up the book that Frankie had given me and started to leaf through the pages. I was stunned to learn that even though the embryo was still quite tadpoley-looking at this stage, there was a lot already taking place inside my body. It was fascinating to see what nature could do. I placed my hands on my stomach and tried to imagine what was going on inside there, and for the first time since I had learned that I was pregnant, I allowed myself to think about my baby's future. I thought of the hopes, dreams, and possibilities that I had for my child and how, no matter what happened, this baby and I were connected together for life.

CHAPTER 36

It was a cold January day and a gust of icy wind rushed through the door whenever it opened. Inside it was cosy, though, with the stove on and the smell of the salted caramel brownies that had just come out of the oven scenting the air. They were divine; when you bit into them, the soft sponge yielded, oozing warm caramel out through the centre. The sharpness of the salt was perfectly complemented by the sweetness of the filling. The taste stayed with you long after the final bite. I knew they wouldn't last too long.

"It smells heavenly in here," Claire said, pushing Ellie over towards the counter. She looked at the plate of steaming brownies. "Oooh, I'll have one of those please, Lily, we're celebrating!"

"Oh, what's the occasion?"

"Ellie slept through the night for the first time!"

"Well done, Ellie," I said, bending down to her pram. "Aren't you a clever girl?" She beamed a smile that would melt the coldest of hearts and I saw that she had cut two teeth since I had last seen her.

"You go get settled over there and I'll bring these over for you."

Claire wheeled the pram over to a chair; her usual spot on the sofa was taken up by an elderly couple. I watched as Ellie curled her little body upwards with her fists held out at each side of her when her mum lifted her out of her pram. I couldn't believe I was going to have one of them. It was so hard to imagine that I was going to be the one reaching for muslin cloths and cleaning up spew or rubbing a tiny back to bring up wind.

If there was one upside in all of this mayhem in my life, it was that things were slowly starting to improve with the bakery. Once again we had had a hectic morning. Things would enter my head and I would scramble to do them before something else that needed to be done would jump in there too and I would have to add it on to my mental checklist. It seemed to have happened overnight. I was at a loss as to why it had occurred so suddenly, but over the last few days we were starting to get busier and busier. I noticed we seemed to be getting lots of young, glamorous girls through the door. They all had big heads of hair extensions, carefully contoured faces and wore impossibly high heels. At first, I had thought it was what I had termed "the cronut effect" but these girls never ordered food. And I knew it couldn't have been from the leaflets I had dropped into the offices either because they were all schoolgirls. I was starting to grow hopeful that maybe word of mouth had finally started to spread. Whatever it was, I was relieved – finally, I could see a future for my bakery.

The lunchtime rush had just quieted down in favour of the slower pace of the afternoon, when Clara breezed in the door with the two boys on either side of her.

"Clara!" I said, plastering a smile on my face. "Hi, Jacob, hi, Joshua."

"Hi, Auntie Lily," they chorused.

"You look nice!" Jacob said.

"Do I? Thanks, Jacob, I can always rely on you for a compliment," I said, bending down to him. "Come here and give me a hug." There weren't many things that I liked about Clara, but she had made two fabulous little people.

He pulled back and studied me again. He had a look of confusion on his face, like his little brain was busy trying to work something out.

"Are you okay, Jacob?" I said.

"But you look good –"

"You don't need to look so surprised," I said, laughing.

"But Mummy said you're messy –"

"Your Mummy said what?"

"She said you're messy," he repeated. "She said Lily is such a mess."

"Oh, did she now!" I said, putting my hands on my hips and swinging around to face Clara.

"Oh, he must have heard me wrong," she said with a nervous laugh. "I think what I said was 'Lily said yes,' isn't that right, sweetheart?"

He shook his head vigorously. "No, you said to Daddy that 'Lily is such a mess.'"

"That is quite enough now, Jacob," she hissed. "It's time for your piano lessons anyway . . . Look, the reason I'm here is that I just wanted to drop these off –" She let a stack of books fall onto the counter with a thud. "They're guides to nutrition during pregnancy. You're laying down the foundations for your

217

child's future health now, so it's important to get it right."

I plastered a smile on my face. "Well, considering I spend a good part of the day throwing up and then when I finally can eat, it's usually cake, I think my child is screwed."

She looked at me in horror. "Don't be flippant, Lily." She pulled the boys' heads into her tummy and covered their ears. "So, did you tell Sam yet?"

"I haven't got around to it . . ."

"Oh, you're just soooo busy here, aren't you?" She looked around the café, which for the first time all day only had two customers. "You're far too busy to take care of a little detail like letting your child's father know that he is actually going to be a father!" She shook her head despairingly at me. "Oh, Lily," she sighed. "Will you ever get it together?"

I decided to fight fire with fire and turn the questions back on her. "So, how's your detective work going? Have you uncovered anything more?"

"Boys, run into the kitchen there and give Granddad a hand," Clara said before turning back to me when they had left. "Well, yes actually, I have!" she pronounced proudly.

"Really?" I asked wide-eyed.

"Tom was in London for work last week and I found a receipt for cocktails. He told me he went to bed straight after dinner. And he came home with a leather jacket – if that's not a sign, then I don't know what is!"

Clara had a point; I couldn't imagine Tom in a leather jacket. He was too much of a fuddy-duddy; he would look ridiculous.

"Why don't you just ask him what's going on, Clara?" I knew she was hurting, but she was causing all this unnecessary drama in her life.

I saw a wobble in her composure. "I can't –" she said quickly.

"Of course, you can, you've done enough digging – it's time to confront him now."

"But what if he admits to it?" There was a flicker of fear behind her eyes.

"Clara, it doesn't have to be the end, if you confront him and he admits to it, you can still work it out if you both want to – " I placed my hand over hers.

She lowered her voice to a whisper. "But what if he doesn't want to? I don't want the boys to come from a broken home."

It was then that I realised her bravado and scheming was all a front. Her investigation into Tom's affairs was her way of taking control of the situation. We were more alike than she thought; we were both afraid to face up to our problems out of fear of being hurt.

CHAPTER 37

"I think I'm going to head to bed," I said to Frankie that evening as she poured herself a large glass of wine.

"Are you sure you're okay, Lily?" I knew she was worried about me.

I nodded. "I'm exhausted."

"You're growing toenails this week apparently."

"Were you reading the book again?"

She nodded. "I can't help it; I'm fascinated by the whole thing. It's amazing; you're amazing." She paused before continuing. "Look, all this stress isn't good for you or the baby. You need to call Sam!"

"But he probably won't even answer anyway!"

"There are other ways – you could email him or text him, you know?"

"I don't want to do it like that –"

"Well, you can't put it off forever, you'll be out of the first trimester soon. Suppose Sam comes home and sees that you are pregnant? Or what if Marita sees you somewhere and tells him? He might never forgive you!"

"I will tell him, I just don't know when . . ." I hugged my knees against my chest.

"What are you afraid of?"

"That he will reject me – reject our baby," I said in a small voice. "I don't think I could cope with that on top of everything else right now."

"He might not react like you think he will," she said.

"But what if he does?" I said in a small voice.

I went to bed that night and fell into a coma-like sleep, but it felt like just seconds later my alarm was blaring, calling me to get up and go to work. As I pulled myself out of bed, I was tired right down into my bones; my body felt like it was wading through a vat of treacle. I had to stop and get sick twice as I tried to get myself ready. My morning sickness was showing no signs of abating. I still felt horrific, but usually by eleven I started to feel more like myself again. I didn't know how I was going to get through the day especially when things were so hectic in *Baked with Love*. It was brilliant to be busy at last, but it was non-stop.

I kept thinking about my conversation with Frankie the evening before. I knew she was right, but it was so hard to work up the courage to tell him. If he rejected me, that was it, I was going to be doing this solo, and I was scared. It was almost easier to be in the mental limbo where I now was and believe there was a chance, even if it was just a small chance that Sam would want to give our relationship another go for the sake of our baby. I had tried rehearsing in my head how I was going to break it to him. Sam, I know this will come as a shock but I'm pregnant or would I be better off just getting directly to the point, Sam, we're going to have a baby?

What way was he going to react? I really hoped he wouldn't get angry. I knew I wouldn't be able to cope with that on top of my own feelings.

While Dad cleared down tables, I stood in the kitchen after the lunchtime rush had died down. I had my phone in my hand. Maybe Frankie was right, Sam was a good person. So he might not want to be with me, but wouldn't he want to be involved in his child's life? I needed to let him know, and then it was up to him to decide what he wanted to do.

I picked up my phone and took a deep breath. I dialled his number and listened to the foreign dial tone as I waited for the phone to be picked up. My throat felt dry and scratchy, and my chest started to tighten. My hands grew clammy around the phone. The phone continued to ring, and my heart was hammering. Eventually I heard the sound of his deep voice. "Hi, this is Sam, please leave a message."

"Sam, it's me – I em . . . I –"

Nothing was coming. The words were stuck in my throat. This wasn't the way I wanted it to be, to have him learn that he was going to be a dad by listening to a stuttering and stammering voicemail. I quickly ended the call.

CHAPTER 38

That night I dreamt I was lying on the grass with my mum. We were sitting on a picnic rug, making daisy chains together in the garden. The sun was high in the sky, and the air was filled with sound of birds chirping and insects humming as they flitted from flower to flower. Mum made a chain for me, and then she handed me a tiny one and said, "That's for the baby."

I woke with a start; my heart was racing. I peeled my eyes open and looked around me. My mood sank when I realised that I wasn't in the garden and instead I was in Frankie's spare room. It had seemed so real. I expected to still be lying there under the warm sunlight with her beside me. Because I had no memories of her, I loved dreaming about her, but then reliving the fact that she was no longer with me when I woke up again always stung. I lay there on the pillow and tried to recall the dream before it vanished entirely from my memory. She knew about the baby, it was as if she was giving me her blessing to say that I could do it – that I would be okay.

I could hear the sound of bells and suddenly I realised they were coming from my phone, which was ringing on the table beside the bed. It vibrated off the locker and onto the floor. I reached out of the bed and felt around on the carpet for it before picking it up and answering it without bothering to check who it was.

"Hello?" I said sleepily. I looked at the red display on my alarm and saw it was just after eight a.m.

"Lily, it's me, Clara –"

My first thought was that Clara ringing me first thing on a Saturday morning was never going to be good news.

"What is it? What's wrong?" I said quickly. I wondered if she had finally confronted Tom.

"Are you not up yet?"

"Well, clearly I am now."

"Have you seen the papers?"

"No, why?"

"You are all over them kissing Marc."

"What?" I said in total disbelief. "I couldn't be –"

"Well, you are, and you should consider wearing high-rise jeans or else spanx in the future."

I was totally lost. "I don't understand . . . what you are talking about?"

"The Irish World paper – you're in their glossy magazine gallivanting with Marc."

"I am not!" I said indignantly.

"I bloody well know what my own sister looks like! I don't know why you would be so stupid as to go back to Marc. I wouldn't usually buy such a rag of a paper, but Tom arrived home with it – probably so he'd have something to talk about with his hussy," she hissed into the phone. "I suggest you go and get yourself a copy."

I hung up and quickly climbed out of bed. I got into the shower and let the water wake me up. I threw on jeans and a

226

sweatshirt and pushed my feet into my trainers. I peeped in on Frankie but she was comatose, so I crept softly out of the apartment and hurried to the nearest shop.

Once there, I ran inside and headed straight for the magazine stand. Neon fonts assailed me and then suddenly a bright pink headline caught my eye.

'MARC EMBRACES MYSTERY WOMAN. IS THIS THE LATEST WOMAN HE IS CHEATING ON NADIA WITH?'

It was a different magazine than the one Clara was talking about. I quickly lifted it down from the stand and was horrified to see that somebody had taken a picture of Marc leaning in to kiss me the day he had called into *Baked with Love*; however, from the angle that it was taken from, it made it look as though we were actually kissing. My top had risen up and you could see my love handles peeking out under the sides. I wanted to die on the spot. With trembling hands, I flicked through the magazine until I got to the story.

Serial womaniser Marc is finding comfort in the arms of a new woman while Nadia is left holding the baby. A clearly strained Nadia, whose on-off relationship has been a source of turmoil for the leading actress, was pictured recently fleeing from the Dublin home they jointly shared together.

There was a photo of a stressed-looking Nadia cradling baby Marley to shield him from the photographer while she hurried down the steps of their home. It was clearly taken a while ago because Marley was much younger in it, but they had stitched the article together to make it look like something it

227

wasn't. I was shaking. I checked the date and saw that it had been published a few days ago. I felt mortified that the copies had been sitting there for the world to see and I didn't even know a thing about it. I checked in a few other gossip magazines and sure enough they had all featured the story. Who would have taken that photo and how did it end up on the front cover of a magazine? Then I thought about Sam and felt panic rise within me. What would he think if he saw it? I knew there was a slim chance he would see it in New York, but what if his family or friends saw it and told him about it? How was I ever going to get him to believe me? And I still had to face telling him that I was pregnant too. This painted a very bad picture, but it was all spin. I realised how it must look to a reader, let alone Nadia, Sam, and everyone else in my life. And what was the most worrying thing of all was that I couldn't stop people from seeing it. I could buy all the copies off this newsstand, but I couldn't scour every shop in Ireland.

I bought the magazine and hurried back to the apartment. Frankie was sitting at the table in her dressing gown, her auburn hair was pulled back in a low ponytail, and her eyes were tired. Her skin looked pale and blotchy. I had noticed two empty bottles of wine sitting beside the recycling bin on my way out the door. She must have polished off both of them after I went to bed.

I placed the magazine in front of her. "What's this?" she asked.

"Look at it," I said.

She read the cover and her hands flew up towards her

228

mouth. "Oh my God, Lily! When did this happen?"

"It didn't! Oh God, if you even think it's true, then I really have no chance of convincing people that it's all a set-up. I was just giving him a hug!"

"I'm not going to lie, it looks really bad . . ."

"What am I going to do?" I wailed. "What if Sam sees it? He already has hang-ups about Marc and me! He'll never believe that it wasn't like that –" I had been dreading telling him that I was pregnant. This would make everything so much worse. He wouldn't want to have anything more to do with me ever again, and I couldn't say I blamed him.

Dad rang me next. "Clara told me what happened. They're an awful shower, those, what do you call them? Pepper-atsy? Have they no regard for the lives of ordinary people? When you think of what they put poor Princess Diana through . . ."

I was hardly in the same league as Princess Diana, but I knew the point he was trying to make. "It looks so bad, Dad, but it wasn't like that –"

"Sure, I was there with you. I saw with my own two eyes that it wasn't like that!"

"You're the only one who knows the truth." No one was going to believe that it was entirely innocent. It looked so much worse than it was. My heart sank.

I lifted the magazine again and stared at the picture for the millionth time trying to figure out where the photo was taken.

"It looks like it was taken on someone's phone," Frankie said, studying it over my shoulder.

"But who would have taken it? Surely none of the

229

customers who had been in *Baked with Love* that day would have been remotely interested in snapping a picture of me hugging Marc? They would have seen it was an innocent hug, so how did they manage to catch that exact moment?"

"Well, unless Marc did it –"

"What do you mean?"

"Well, maybe Marc set the whole thing up?"

"But why would he do that?" Frankie's theory didn't make any sense to me.

"Oh, I don't know – to get a bit of publicity?"

"You think?"

"He's desperate for money plus he's so hungry for fame that he doesn't care how he gets it. Good or bad publicity – it's all the same to him."

Suddenly, it was starting to make sense. Marc was hardly famous enough that he would have the paparazzi following him around; however, if he sold them a staged photo and handed them a salacious story on a plate in exchange for a few quid, then surely it was a no brainer for them to run it and help shift a few copies.

"So you think he tipped off the magazines?" I said, Frankie's theory finally clicking into the place.

"Well, yeah, or else he got someone to take the photo for him and sold it onto them for a bit of cash."

"But what about Nadia?"

"They've broken up, haven't they?"

"Yeah, but –"

"Well, wouldn't this be the ultimate revenge?"

"Would he really be that stupid?" I asked in disbelief.

She looked at me with narrowed eyebrows, and we both laughed.

"It's the only explanation, Lily," she continued.

Suddenly, I knew she was right. My stomach flipped and started to knot. I felt a wave of nausea grow inside me. It was one thing if somebody took a photo unbeknownst to either of us, but if Marc had been the one to stage the photo, using me to get a bit of publicity and risk damaging my relationship with Sam, then it was sickening. Did our history mean nothing to him that he could use me so carelessly as a pawn in his games? Hadn't he caused enough trouble for me?

CHAPTER 39

I was grateful to be flat out all the next day; it meant I had less time to spend worrying over how I was going to tell Sam. I would be busy clearing tables when I would see Dad falling behind with the queue, so I would have to run and give him a hand. I was glad to see the huge piles of cakes I had stocked that morning were rapidly dwindling, although it would mean I would have less left over to give to Father Joe, I thought guiltily. I had just wiped down a table and was bringing the plates into the kitchen when I found my path blocked by a girl taking a selfie. She was just like all the others; long hair extensions cascaded down her back, her make-up emphasised pouty lips, and she wore scarily high heels.

"Sorry," I said, trying to move around her.

She glared at me for daring to interrupt her, then walked over and sat down, tossing her voluminous mane of hair over her shoulder.

I hurried past her and into the kitchen, my arms laden with the weight of crockery. I couldn't understand why we had got so busy all of a sudden. Why were my customers all the same type of girl? And what was the obsession with taking selfies? They never ordered the sweet stuff; it was always just coffee. Although our coffee was good, I didn't think it was that much of a draw. Don't get me wrong, I wasn't complaining, I just wanted to understand what was bringing them in the door so I could use it to get more customers.

I opened the dishwasher and steam rushed out. I began to unload it, before I would fill it once again. It seemed to be working around the clock now. As I stacked the clean plates on top of each other, it suddenly dawned on me. It was so obvious! Why hadn't I realised earlier? The reason that all these young girls were coming in was because they had seen the magazines. They thought *Baked with Love* was some new cool celeb hangout. I put the plates down with a clatter as the realization hit me. I leaned back against the worktop and groaned. I was glad to have the extra business, but I had believed that all my hard work was finally paying off. I had stupidly thought that my cronuts had put *Baked with Love* on the map. I assumed word of mouth was spreading about town, but instead it was because some teenage girls thought they might get a chance spot a Z-list actor. Suddenly, I felt rage coursing through my veins. I tossed my tea towel down on the bench in anger. Bloody Marc, would I ever be free of him?

When I got home to the apartment that evening, I flung my handbag onto the worktop.

"Frankie?" I called out.

"I'm in here," her voice replied from the bathroom.

I made my way in to where she was applying thick eyeliner in the mirror. I went and sat on the side of the bathtub and talked to her reflection.

"You're heading out?"

"There's a launch for a new line of hosiery called 'Second

Skin,' want to come?" she asked, turning away from the mirror.

I wasn't in the mood for going out socializing. "I think I'll pass, Frankie."

"So, did you tell Sam?" she asked, turning back and concentrating hard on applying her eyeliner.

"You know I didn't," I said.

"Well, you might get around to doing it before the child starts school." She stuck out her tongue at me in the mirror.

"So, I finally figured out where all my customers are coming from," I said, changing the subject.

"Oh yeah?" she said, carefully angling the brush to paint a flick.

"Well, they've seen the magazines, haven't they? They reckon it's a new celeb hangout."

She swung around from the mirror; her eyes were wide. "You're right!"

"And there was me getting all excited because I thought I'd done it through all my own hard work."

"Don't get deflated, Lily. There's no such thing as bad publicity!"

I shrugged my shoulders. "I guess . . ."

"Look, it's happened now so try to use it to your advantage. These new people will spread the word. It all helps. Right, I have to run," she said, leaning in to kiss me on the cheek.

* * *

I went to bed that night and let my body sink into the weight of the mattress. I was bone tired, and I was asleep before my head

235

even touched the pillow.

I woke a while later to someone calling my name and a loud bang, I startled and sat up in the bed. Then I heard another bang. I listened out but I couldn't figure out where it was coming from. I rubbed my eyes and looked across to the alarm clock. The red glow of the LED told me it was 4.03 a.m.

"Lily – help me!" The voice said again. I suddenly realised that it was coming from Frankie's room. "Lily!" Her voice was growing more frantic.

I hurried out of bed and ran out to the hall. I screamed when I saw a man standing in the hallway, banging on Frankie's bedroom door.

"Open the bloody door!" he was roaring at her.

"Stop it!" I screamed at him. He didn't even turn and look at me; he was too intent on breaking down her bedroom door. "Frankie – are you okay?" I shouted to her in panic.

He continued pummelling on the door with his fist while I ran out to the kitchen and started flinging open the cupboard doors, looking for something I could use to hit him. I found a saucepan and ran back in to where he was still pounding on the door. I lifted up the saucepan and held it up high above my head. Then I closed my eyes and lowered my hands down until I felt it connect with his body. I dared to open my eyes and saw him grip his shoulder in agony. He spun around to face me. "What the fuck did you do that for?" His eyes were blazing, and suddenly, I was frightened. I raised the saucepan over my head again. "Go on, get out of here," I said.

"Stupid bitch – a prick tease is all she is!"

236

"Now, you just hold on a minute –" I raised my saucepan higher.

"Don't worry, I'm going now –" He turned and went to walk past me towards the door.

And then before I knew what I was doing I drew back the saucepan and planted a blow squarely on his other shoulder.

He stumbled forward knocking a vase off its table where it smashed into jagged pieces all over the floor.

"Jesus, you're a right pair of fucking crazy bitches!" he said, picking himself up off the floor.

"Go on, get out," I ordered.

He stumbled dizzily towards the door, rubbing his other shoulder with his hand. I watched as he made his way down the corridor towards the lift, clumsily hitting off the walls as he walked. Doors began to open as neighbours with sleepy heads and wrapped dressing gowns came out into the corridor, obviously having been woken by the ruckus and wanting to know what was going on.

"Sorry," I mouthed in apology.

When the lift doors closed, I shut the front door and put the keychain across it just in case.

"It's okay, Frankie," I called out. "He's gone now."

The bedroom door opened, and Frankie ran out and into my arms. "Oh, Lily!" she started to sob. I guided her into the living room and sat her down on the sofa. She was crying hysterically. Frankie never cried.

"Oh, Lily, I'm sorry - I was so scared –" she said breathlessly.

"What happened, Frankie? What was he doing here?"

"He's a guy I met in town –" she started to sob. "The rest of the crew cried off after eleven, but I didn't want to go home, so I got chatting to him at the bar. We were just talking and having a laugh – so I invited him back here for a few drinks. We were having the craic, and he went to kiss me. And I don't know what happened – one minute, I was fine, and the next I felt dizzy, so I pulled back, but he kept on at me. He was trying to take off my top, but I wanted him to stop, I needed air, so I got up off the sofa. But he got really mad and started shouting at me, and then he pushed me back down again and got on top of me. I was so frightened, Lily – I managed to slide out from underneath him and make a run for it, but he pinned me against the wall. I was able to duck under his arm, and I ran into the bedroom. He started banging on the door then and shouting horrible things at me. That's when I screamed for you. If you hadn't been staying here it could have been so different –"

"You had a lucky escape, honey." I shuddered to think what might have happened if she had been alone. She was shaking violently, so I took the throw off the couch and put it around her shoulders. I got up and put the kettle on and made us both a mug of sweet tea.

"Here, get this into you," I said, handing her a mug.

I knew that if I was any sort of friend to Frankie I couldn't ignore the elephant in the room any longer. I sat down beside her and took a deep breath.

"Look, Frankie, do you think maybe you've been overdoing it a bit lately?" I said softly.

238

"How do you mean?"

"I'm not saying what happened tonight was your fault – he was a nasty creep – but for your own safety, you should have left at the same time as your friends rather than staying behind on your own just so you could drink more. You're going to have to cut back on what you're drinking. I didn't want to say anything to you before, but lately you just seem to spend your days going from one drunken daze to the next."

She was silent for what seemed like forever.

"Oh, Lily –" she said eventually and the tears started to spill down her face until she could barely catch her breath. "I'm such a mess."

"Here, you're okay, let it all out. You got a terrible fright tonight."

"I know I'm drinking too much, but I don't know . . . it's like I can't stop."

"You can, Frankie – this is a wake-up call for you. I will help you get through this."

"I got such a fright tonight, Lily – I always thought I was okay with alcohol, y'know? I never used to drink on my own, and I would have the same amount as everyone else on nights out, but lately . . . I don't know what's come over me. It started off with me having a glass of wine after a long day in work, then the next night I wouldn't want the bottle to go off, so I'd have another. Then the next night I'd have another really stressful day, so I'd allow myself one but now it's got to the stage where I can't face an evening without a drink. It's my way to relax – I tell myself I deserve it. It is my reward for a hard day. I've started coming home from nights out and having nightcaps by myself, which I know is bad – that's why I asked that guy back earlier on – you don't feel guilty if someone else is drinking with you because you're just being social. I guess when I'm drinking I don't feel so alone . . . I know it sounds pathetic."

"But you have me –" I was shocked by her admission.

"As much as I love you, I'd like something more . . ."

"But I thought you loved being single?"

"I did, but it's been years now, I think it would be nice to have someone to come home to."

"But you're not on your own, I'm living with you now?"

"You have the baby, even if you and Sam never get it together, you and the baby will be a family. I feel like everyone else's life is moving on, whereas mine is just static."

"Why didn't you say anything to me before, Frankie?" I rubbed the back of her hand.

"Well, it's not really the kind of thing you can just drop into conversation. Since you found out that you were pregnant, it really hit me that my own life is so empty . . ." She fell silent, then whispered, "I swore I would never let drink control me and ruin my life the way it did for my dad, and now look at me?" She shook her head despairingly. "I'm pathetic."

"No you're not," I said. "And you won't turn out like your Dad because you're already facing up to it."

"I can't believe how close I was to going down the same road though, and I never saw it coming. It scares me how history is repeating itself. I was so angry with Dad growing up, how he wasted his life in and out of treatment centres . . . and then this has been creeping up on me and I didn't even notice it!" She turned to look at me with frightened eyes.

"At least you can see what's happening, and now you can change it before you go down the same road as he did. I'm not going to let that happen to you – no way. It's all going to be okay."

* * *

I tiptoed out of the apartment quietly the next morning and left Frankie tucked up in bed. She needed the sleep after the events of the night before. She had got a nasty fright, but I hoped this would be a wake-up call for her. She needed to get her drinking under control.

It seemed that from the moment I opened the doors of *Baked with Love* that morning we had a queue. Frankie had said that there was no such thing as bad publicity, and I guess she was right. Yes, I had lots of young celeb spotters through the doors, but I had lots of other customers too. I had started to notice a lot of the same faces returning again and bringing new people with them, which made me feel so proud that they were spreading the word about *Baked with Love*. Finally, the business was getting the traction that I knew in my heart and soul it deserved. And if somebody complimented one of my cakes, I felt like a new mother must feel when somebody stops to admire her baby. Whenever a queue would form, although good for business, my heart would start beating a bit faster as I worked my way down the line trying to serve people efficiently so they wouldn't get impatient.

I enjoyed the rhythm of the day. The ebb and flow of

customers, the morning-time tsunami of coffee to go, the calm but steady stream in the afternoon. As I went about my work, I couldn't help but think about what had happened the previous evening. The whole thing had got me thinking: Frankie wasn't the only one who needed to face up to things. I needed to take a leaf out of my own book and stop running away from my problems. It was time to tell Sam. I knew he wouldn't answer my calls to his mobile, so I decided to ring him in work. When we had a quiet spell in the afternoon, I left Dad front of house and went back into the kitchen. With trembling hands, I picked up my phone and dialled his office number.

"Hello, First Ireland Bank, how can I direct your call?" a woman sang in an American accent.

I took a deep breath. "Hi, can I speak with Sam Waters please?"

"Let me put you through to his P.A."

Sam had his own P.A. now? He really was a hotshot. I felt a sting for all I was missing out on. I was proud of him for being so successful but sad that I was no longer there to share it with him.

I was transferred to a woman with a southern drawl.

"I'd like to speak to Sam Waters please," I said.

"And who should I say is calling?" She sounded so upbeat and chirpy in total contrast to my own feelings.

I guessed that he probably had warned her not to put me through, so although I hated lying, I knew I would have to use a fake name if I had any chance of speaking to him. "It's . . . um . . . Irene –"

"Okay, you just hold the line there please, Irene."

The phone was answered moments later. "Hello, Sam speaking –"

The familiar sound of his voice caused my nerves to ratchet up again. It had been so long since we had last talked. My heart ached for him.

"Sam – it's me, Lily."

"Lily? What the hell do you want? I told you not to call me!"

"Wait! Please don't hang up. I'm sorry for using a fake name, but I knew you wouldn't have taken the call and I really need to talk to you –"

"Well, I don't think there's anything left to say –"

"Please, Sam – it's important –"

"I'm trying to get on with my life, Lily – please, can't you just let me do that?"

I knew I had to do this now before he hung up on me. "I have some news for you –" My heart was hammering with every word that left my mouth.

"Look, I'm in a new relationship now –" he cut across me. "I've moved on, Lily, and you should too –"

My heart fell with a tremendous thud as the words scalded and stung. He had somebody new in his life already? It hadn't taken him long to move on. How was I ever meant to tell him that I was pregnant now?

"I – I – see," I stuttered. "I – I – I hope you'll be very happy together," I said hanging up the phone.

CHAPTER 40

This was the part when I realised that real life wasn't like the movies. In all the times over the last few weeks that I had tried to envisage how the conversation might play out, that was not how I had imagined it going. I had expected shock, maybe even anger, but certainly not to be told that he was in a relationship with someone new before I had even managed to get the words out. I knew a small part inside of me had hoped that when I did finally pluck up the courage to tell Sam that he would have been happy to learn he was going to be a dad. I had secretly wished that he would say we could work it out for the sake of the baby and give our relationship another try, but the phone call had ended with him telling me he had found happiness in the arms of someone new before I had even had a chance to tell him my news. I guess I had watched one too many rom-coms.

Frankie and I had drunk mug after mug of tea chatting about it that evening. Although she was still recovering from her ordeal, her outlook on life was already more positive. I think admitting how unhappy she was had been a weight off her mind, and now she could start building a path towards getting herself well again.

"So, you didn't get to tell him?" Frankie asked as I recounted the conversation to her.

I shook my head. "When I heard that he had somebody

new, I just couldn't. I was in shock -"

"I'm so sorry, honey," she soothed.

"I can't believe he was ready to jump into a new relationship so soon. There's no way I could even look at another man right now! He was so cold on the phone, you should have heard him, Frankie . . . I just thought I meant more to him than that . . ."

"He's on the rebound, Lily, it won't last."

"You don't know that though, do you?"

"You still need to tell him about the baby, even if he's with someone new, he still has duties to you both."

"I know," I sighed.

I didn't sleep at all that night. I tossed and turned in Frankie's spare room until I finally pulled myself out of bed at three a.m. It was pointless just lying there with my head running in a constant loop of worries and hurt. I went out to the kitchen and switched on the lights under the cupboards, bathing the kitchen in a soft glow. I went to the press and automatically started pulling out flour and eggs. It was like a magnetic force pulling me towards it. Baking was the only thing I knew that would help to take my mind off my worries and calm me down. As my fingers worked their way through the buttery dough, I could feel my whole body start to relax. I added some vanilla extract and, when I was finished, put the mixture into the oven. Soon the sweet smell had scented the whole apartment. I made myself a coffee and went into the living room. I saw the photo of Mam staring down at me from Frankie's bookshelves. It was one of my most treasured possessions; I brought it everywhere I went. I loved studying her face; I always found something different that I hadn't noticed before. Sometimes it would be the gradual arch of her eyebrows or the gentle slope of her nose. Having no memories of her, studying her face was the only way I could get to know her. It was at times like this that I missed her desperately. I envied people who still had their mothers around and could turn to them for advice when things were falling apart.

I picked it up in my hands. "Oh, Mam," I sighed with tears tripping my voice. "Why does it have to be so hard? I know I've made a mess of things lately – well, 'mess' is probably putting it mildly, but I'm working on it, I really am. I'm going to get my life together, make you proud of me again. I promise," I whispered to her photo.

CHAPTER 41

Soon dawn began to break over the city. The sky shifted from shades of pink to blue, and I could hear the city coming to life below as the sound of a jackhammer began digging up the road as I started to get ready for work. The lack of sleep had left my body aching all over, and even my skin hurt as the water ran over me in the shower. I was beginning to think I was coming down with something. I managed only to get sick once that morning though, so I was trying to count my blessings.

It was a sunny spring day as I threw open the door of *Baked with Love* that morning. And it wasn't long before the café was filled with the sound of chatter and clinking china. I looked out the window and saw that beyond, people were thronging the streets looking cheerful. All the tables I had put outside that morning were now full. We so rarely got good weather in Ireland that as soon as the sun came out, people wanted to make the most of it. I had rugs for people to throw over their laps in case they grew chilly, and people seemed to like it.

We were doing a roaring trade in boxes of mini mint and raspberry cheesecakes, which I had displayed by the till. They were fresh and summery and proving really popular. People were in a good mood and wanted to treat themselves.

I, however, felt as though I was dragging myself around all

day. Whenever I thought about Sam in New York and his new girlfriend I felt so sad. I was now realizing that deep down I had never really believed that our relationship was over; I had always thought there was unfinished business and that we'd get to sort it out one day, so to hear that he had moved on without me was devastating. I was only now accepting that our relationship was truly finished. As I thought about the two of them together, I couldn't help but wonder if they were at that stage where they couldn't keep their hands off one another. Were they experiencing that insatiable desire where they were on each other's mind constantly? I remembered the frisson of the early stages when we were together, and I felt distraught that someone else was experiencing that with him now. Did he even think about me anymore? And how on earth was I supposed to tell him about the baby now?

"Here, don't be lifting that in your condition," Dad said, wrestling a chair out of my hands. "You need to be taking it a bit easier."

I was too tired to protest, and I put it back down again. My legs felt like they had been cast in concrete as I moved around *Baked with Love*.

"Are you sure you're okay, love?" Dad asked for what felt like the hundredth time.

"I'm fine, Dad, I just didn't sleep great."

"She's looking very peaky all right," Mabel said, joining the queue with little Lottie.

"Hi, Mabel. I'm fine, you two, now stop fussing! Will I get you the usual?" Mabel had become partial to my spiced pear tart over recent weeks.

"Please, Lily love."

"Me want honey cookie," Lottie shouted. Then remembered her manners. "Please," she added with a sweet smile.

Mabel and Lottie sat down, and Dad got their order ready and brought it over to them. He stood chatting with Mabel for a few minutes while Lottie was colouring. I watched them as they talked; he had a smile stretching from ear to ear. They really seemed to have hit it off.

The rest of the day went past in endless cappuccinos, teas, chatting to customers, snapping on latex gloves, peeling off latex gloves, slicing cake, mixing more cake batter, cleaning up, checking stock levels, reordering supplies, more cleaning, paying invoices before getting ready to do it all again the next day.

I still wasn't feeling well and couldn't face the cycle home, so I decided to get a taxi.

When I reached Frankie's apartment, the smell of melted cheese greeted me from outside the door and made me want to vomit.

"I made this for you," Frankie said, lifting a steaming dish from the oven as soon as I came into the kitchen. "Comfort food."

I looked at the lasagne, still bubbling in its dish and gagged.

"Sorry," I said. "The baby says no –"

"It's okay – I'll forgive you."

251

I sank down onto the sofa and took a quick look around to see if there was a wine glass anywhere like there usually would be when I came home, but true to her word there was none. I knew it wasn't easy for her and I was proud of her.

"So how are you doing?" she asked.

"I can't believe it's over, y'know? I think in the back of my mind I always believed that we'd work it out . . ."

"So did you decide when you're going to tell him about the baby? Who knows, maybe when his new girlfriend hears she might run a mile?" she said with a wry smile.

"It's such a mess." I sighed.

"How are you feeling today?"

"Shit."

"You'll start feeling better any day now; you're nearly at week twelve and the placenta will be taking over soon, mark my words."

"Have you been reading the book again?"

"Maybe . . ." she said, grinning at me.

I smiled back at her. I just knew she was going to be right by my side every step of the way, and I was so glad to have a friend like her.

"So I heard something today that might put a smile on your face –" she continued.

"Go on –"

"Well, the make-up artist that was doing the shoot today works with Nadia a good bit and apparently she has finally wised up to Marc! She had given him so many chances for Marley's sake, but apparently after seeing that story, she went

252

crazy. I can't say I blame her, so she threw him out, sold his car, changed all the locks, and she's cut off his access to her money and everything. And the best bit is that nobody in the industry will hire him because of what he did to her!"

"Wow," I said, but the news didn't make me feel any better about my own situation instead I just felt even more depressed.

"What's wrong? I thought that would cheer you up," Frankie asked.

"I'm sorry, I'm not feeling so good. I think I'm going to go straight to bed." My whole body was aching and I was finding it hard to keep my eyes open.

I woke some time later needing to use the bathroom. My tummy was cramping, and I didn't feel well at all. I pulled myself up and sat against the pillows. I tried to figure out what time it was; I was disorientated. I got up and went into the toilet – that was another crazy pregnancy symptom – the amount of times I had to use the toilet. I flicked on the light, and it was then that I saw it; bright red blood stained my pyjama bottoms. I stood still, I was too afraid to move in case I made whatever was happening worse.

"Frankie?" I called out, hoping she would hear me through the wall.

After a few seconds, I heard her stumbling out of bed. She entered the bathroom bleary-eyed as her eyes tried to adjust to the light.

"What is it, Lily?"

"I'm bleeding –" My voice came out in a whisper.

"The baby?" she asked, suddenly waking up.

253

I nodded. "I think so . . . oh, Frankie I'm scared," I whispered.

CHAPTER 42

Frankie drove us the short distance to the maternity hospital. She broke red lights, zipped up bus lanes, and undertook other cars that weren't going fast enough. I looked out at the city lights as they whizzed past the window of her mini cooper.

"It'll all be okay, Lily," she said, reaching across the gearstick to squeeze my hand when we were stopped at a junction.

I stayed quiet beside her. I was terrified to speak, and I could tell she didn't know what to say to me. For the shock that this baby had been to me, and the turbulence it had caused in my life, I had grown attached to the idea of motherhood even if it meant doing it alone. I didn't want to lose my baby. Over the last few days I had started to allow myself to imagine what our future would be like together. Would it be a boy or girl? Would they be fair like me or more olive-skinned like Sam? What would his or her first word be?

Frankie parked outside the door and put on her hazard lights. The night porter directed us to the emergency room where a kindly midwife took my details and told me to take a seat.

"It'll be okay," Frankie said, giving me a reassuring squeeze again.

There were other women seated under the bright fluorescent lights of the emergency room, some were in the early stages just like me, others were further along. Nobody dared to speak; we were too caught up in our own worries. The one thing that united us was that we were all anxious for our babies.

Eventually, we were called. "Lily McDermott?"

I entered the darkened room, followed closely by Frankie. The hum of the sonography equipment filled the air.

I held my breath as the sonographer squeezed cool gel across my stomach before scanning me with the probe. Her forehead was creased in concentration. I tried to study her reactions because the screen just seemed to be a blur of black and white. It felt as though I was waiting an eternity for her to speak.

"I'm sorry, Lily, sometimes these things take a while," she said eventually. "Bear with me."

I swallowed back a sob. Frankie squeezed my hand tightly in hers. This was not good news; she couldn't find a heartbeat. I just knew it.

Eventually, I saw a slow smile break across her face. She clicked on the screen and began dragging lines from left to right.

"You see this, Lily?" she asked.

I looked at a pulsing image on the screen. I nodded, secretly daring to hope that it was what I thought it was.

"That's your baby's heart. Here, do you want to hear it?"

I listened as she pressed a button and soon the cubicle was filled with what sounded like horses' hooves racing over arid land. I don't think I have ever heard a sweeter sound. My heart swelled with love and pride, and before I knew it, I had tears of joy spilling down my face. I looked over at Frankie, and she was grinning manically at me. "Oh, Frankie!" I cried.

"So it's okay then, the baby is okay?" she asked jumping off her chair to take a closer look at the screen.

"The baby looks perfect to me. The heartbeat is good and strong. According to this scan, you're almost twelve weeks along."

"But why was I bleeding then? Does that mean something is wrong with the baby?"

"Sometimes women bleed for no known reason. However, I can see you have a low-lying placenta, which sometimes can be a reason for this sort of thing happening. Have you been under stress lately or doing too much?"

Frankie looked at me and raised her eyebrows.

"Well, yeah, I've had a stressful few weeks . . ."

The sonographer nodded knowingly. "Stress can do funny things to our bodies. You're growing another person now – it's no mean feat. You need to start taking it a bit easier. I'd recommend a few days of rest, and then when you're feeling better, you should think about joining an antenatal yoga class if you find yourself getting stressed. Sometimes things like this happen to give us a little wake-up call; it's our body's way of telling us to take it easy."

The journey home was much calmer. As Frankie drove us through the deserted city streets, we were both quiet as we thought back over the events of the night.

When I climbed back into bed that night, I placed my hands on my abdomen. I was so thankful to still have my little baby here with me. I made a promise to him or her that from then on I was going to be the best mother that I could be. No matter what happened, I vowed to start putting this baby first. It was me and this baby united against the world.

CHAPTER 43

I stayed in bed the next morning and let Frankie attend to me. I had learnt my lesson and was so grateful to still have my baby with me that I wasn't going to jeopardise it again. I knew the stress I had put myself under over the last few weeks had taken its toll and it wasn't good for the baby or me. My life wasn't just about me anymore; I had somebody else to think about too. Although I wished dearly that Sam was by my side, I was slowly learning to accept that I would be doing it alone, and although I was scared, I was summoning strength from somewhere I didn't know I had. Maybe it was from the baby. Together we would be our own unit, and I knew Dad and Frankie would be a great support to me too.

Frankie had left me the remote control and a tray piled high with snacks, all within arm's reach so that I wouldn't have to get out of bed.

"The only time you're allowed out of this bed is to use the toilet," she had warned as she had left for work that morning.

I noticed she had chosen healthy things like flapjacks, and I spied a packet of kale crisps sticking out underneath a bunch of bananas. I never usually had time to watch TV, so I was binge-watching episodes of the Bake Off. I called Dad to check in with *Baked with Love*, and he told me that he and Clara had everything under control. I had finally agreed that since *Baked with Love* was so busy these days that we needed to hire someone else, especially now that I was pregnant. I would need someone to help Dad out while I was at my antenatal appointments and have them trained up for when I would be on maternity leave, and I couldn't always keep asking Clara. I still wasn't sure how that was all going to work, trying to run a business with a baby in tow, but I decided in my new Zen mindset that I wasn't going to worry about that now. I had to trust that it would all work out as Dad and Frankie, rather annoyingly, kept reminding me.

I spent the day snoozing and watching some TV only broken with trips to the toilet. It was blissful, but when my phone rang and I saw it was Clara, immediately I felt panicked. I hoped nothing was wrong in *Baked with Love*.

"Clara, is everything okay?" I said quickly.

"Don't worry, everything is fine with *Baked with Love*," she whispered. "But I've just come home and I – I can hear people having sex upstairs in my bedroom."

"Oh, Clara, are you sure?" I said stunned. Surely Tom wouldn't be so stupid.

"I know what it sounds like –" She choked back a sob. She sounded desolate, completely unlike her usual brash self. My heart broke for her. Whatever she was going to uncover in her bedroom was going to be horrible, and I didn't want her to face it alone. I had been through it all before, except it was even worse for her because they had two children together, so she had to think of them as well.

"Okay, you stay right there and promise me you won't go

260

up there on your own, I'll be right over." I knew I was supposed to be on bed rest but Clara needed me.

CHAPTER 44

I quickly pulled back the duvet and jumped out of bed. I stuck my feet into my runners and hurried out to the hall. I ran slap bang into Frankie coming in through the door from work.

"And where do you think you're going?" she asked blocking my path with her hands on her hips.

"It's Clara –" I said. "She's just walked in on Tom having sex with someone in their bed!"

"Tom? Really? Euggh, he's about as sexy as a head of cabbage!" She shuddered. "It's always the ones you least expect," she said, shaking her head.

"It's been going on for weeks now, but she has been waiting to confront him about it. It sounds like he's going to get it tonight though."

"That's not all he's getting! How stupid can he be? Doing it on his own doorstep!" She pursed her lips in disgust. "Men – they're all the same, if they thought with their brains more than their penises, they'd go far - wait is it penises or penii?"

"I'm not really sure but it doesn't matter," I said impatiently. "I need to go!"

"Come on, get in the car, I'll drive you over."

"Oh, Frankie, that would be great! Are you sure you don't mind?"

"And miss a ringside seat at the epic showdown of Clara

versus Tom! Are you mad?"

We hurried down to the basement and jumped into Frankie's mini. We drove past the Liffey, so dark and still under the moonlight. Soon we had left the city lights behind us and we were in the leafy suburban streets of Dublin 4. Imposing red-bricked mansions stood proudly on either side of the road fronted by manicured hedges. Eventually, Frankie turned the car into Clara's driveway. I hopped out and entered the code for the automatic gates. When they parted, we drove over the crunchy gravel and came to a stop in front of the house.

Clara met us at the door looking distraught. She put her finger over her lips signaling for us to be quiet. We listened, and sure enough we could hear loud groans coming from upstairs.

"Has he been at it all this time?" I whispered in disbelief. Tom was no spring chicken.

"I have to give it to him – he has some stamina!" Frankie whispered after a minute.

Clara shot her a look. "It's a compliment!" Frankie argued back.

"Where are the boys?" I said, changing the subject.

"At their swimming lessons with Olga. The bastard must have thought I'd still be in the café," she said tearfully.

"I think you'd better go upstairs, Clara," I said softly. "We'll be right with you." I reached for her hand and squeezed it in solidarity.

The three of us threaded the stairs taking care not to make noise. We rounded the return and climbed the rest of the steps until we were on the landing. The groans were getting louder, the closer we got to the bedroom. We tiptoed over Clara's plush carpet until we were right outside the door. Clara took a deep breath before reaching for the handle but then hesitated at the last second.

"I can't –" she whispered, turning around to look at us.

"Here," Frankie said, pushing down on the handle and walking into the room before either of us could stop her. We followed her into the room where hastily removed clothes were strewn across the carpet, but Tom wasn't in the bed. It was a man none of us recognized, and lying beside him was a terrified-looking Olga. They both stayed rooted to the spot like rabbits caught in the headlights.

"Why you here?" Olga screamed at us while trying to cover herself with the sheet.

"I was about to ask you the same thing!" Clara roared. "What do you think you're doing? Where are the boys? You're meant to be bringing them to their swimming lessons!"

"They're with Tom, he come home from work early to take them because you work all day in café," she tried to explain through her broken English.

"Good old, Tom," Clara said with tears glistening in the corners of her eyes. "I should never have doubted him." She shook her head despairingly. "Why are you in my bed? Aren't there other places you could use for your . . . your . . . shenanigans?"

"We like the sex in other people's beds," Olga offered as if it was a reasonable excuse.

I was aghast. Even the normally unflappable Frankie was

staring at her open-mouthed.

"Get out of my bed, Olga, go pack your things, and then I'd like you to leave my house and never come back," Clara hissed.

We watched as Olga got out of bed still trying to cover herself with the sheet while her boyfriend ran behind her trying to cover his manhood with his hands. He quickly grabbed his clothes off the floor and headed straight for the stairs.

"Where do you think you're going with my sheet? That has a 440 thread count you know!" Clara said pulling it off her.

A naked Olga ran off for her bedroom, and we listened through the walls while she made a racket packing up her stuff.

"What's going on?" Tom said, coming into the bedroom moments later with Jacob and Joshua on either side of him. "I met a fella running down the driveway, half-naked! I thought we were being burgled!"

"Oh, Tom, I'm so sorry," Clara said, running up and throwing her arms around him.

"Sorry, for what?" He pulled back and looked at her, his eyebrows raised. "You're not – you're not with that fella, are you?" he asked in disbelief.

She shook her head. "Oh Tom," she started to cry. "I found underwear in our bed a few weeks ago and I thought you were having an affair."

"I would never do that!" he said indignantly.

"I know that now, but you see I found some things that I was sure were proof that you were being unfaithful, so I guess I got carried away –" She wiped her tears with the back of her hand.

"Like what?" Tom asked in bewilderment.

"Well, I found out about your account in the Bahamas –" she said sheepishly.

"That's a trust fund should the worst ever happen to me, Clara. I want you and the boys to be provided for –"

"And then when you came home from London wearing the leather jacket . . ."

"What's wrong with my jacket?" he said, looking affronted.

"Well, it's a bit . . ." she paused to choose the right word, "young for you, don't you think?"

"Oh . . ." Tom said, feeling hurt. "The girl in the shop said it suited me . . ."

"I'm so sorry, Tom," Clara said, throwing her arms around him and collapsing against his chest. "I'm sorry, I should have trusted you."

"You know you're the only woman I love, Clara, it's only ever been you," Tom said.

She nodded. "I know that, Tom, I'm sorry for being such a fool. It turns out that Olga and her boyfriend have been using our bed. When I came home earlier, they were up here."

"What?" Tom said in horror pulling back from her. "But she has her own bed!"

"Why was Olga in your bed, Mummy?" Jacob asked.

"Because it's really bouncy," I said quickly.

Clara hugged the boys' heads towards her chest and covered their ears. "They get a kick out of having sex in other people's beds," she whispered.

Tom's jaw dropped.

"I'm so sorry for doubting you," she said as she relaxed her grip on the boys and rested her head against Tom's shoulder.

We heard someone enter the room moments later and turned around to see Olga standing there with a bulging suitcase beside her feet.

"I sorry Tom and Clara."

Clara nodded.

"Can I get reference for new job?"

We all stood looking at her open-mouthed. I had to hand it to her, she had balls.

"The only reference you'll be getting from me is to tell your new employers to make sure that their bedroom doors are locked!"

"I understand," she said, lowering her gaze to the floor. "I go now, bye, boys." She turned and left the room.

"Bye, Olga," the boys chorused, oblivious to what was going on.

They ran over and jumped up onto the bed and began bouncing up and down.

"Olga was right, this bed is really bouncy!" Jacob squealed.

Clara started to laugh then at the absurdity of the whole thing.

We listened as Olga made her way down the stairs, and when we finally heard the slam of the door, Clara sank down onto the side of bed and sighed. Tom followed her and sat down beside her. "I love you, you daft mare," he said, throwing his arm around her shoulder and giving her a kiss.

I looked at Clara, Tom, and their two boys who were still bouncing up and down on the bed. Clara was laughing and crying, and Tom was soothing her. I looked at the perfect scene before me. I was happy for her that it had all worked out okay, but once again it was a bittersweet reminder that my own child would be lacking this family togetherness from his or her life.

"Come on," Frankie said, missing nothing. She put her arm around me. "Let's get you home."

CHAPTER 45

The next morning I flicked open my eyes and let them adjust to the shocking pink walls. I turned over to check my phone on the locker and startled to see that I wasn't alone. There was someone sitting on the chair beside my bed and I was shocked to see it was Sam. It took a moment for my head to work out if this was reality or if I was still dreaming.

"Hey there," he said, reaching out for my hand. "How are you feeling?"

I rubbed my eyes, hardly daring to believe that it was him. I tried to sit up. "What are you doing here?" was all I could manage.

"Please don't be mad – Frankie let me in. She phoned and told me everything. I came as soon as I could –"

My mind was trying to work out what was going on but it struggled to make sense of it all. "You know about the baby?" I said in disbelief.

He nodded. "Frankie called me and told me you were in the hospital and that you were pregnant. I got such a fright. I had to see you, so I got on the next available flight."

I couldn't believe that Frankie had orchestrated all of this without me knowing it. I felt relieved that Sam knew at last and that the burden of my secret could finally be lifted.

"I don't understand how it happened though?" he

continued. "I thought you were on the pill –"

I had had the same reaction when I had first learned that I was pregnant, and I knew the shock that he was going through right now as his brain tried to process everything that was being said. "I guess we're one of the one percent that it doesn't work for . . ."

"So how long have you known for?"

"Just over a month now."

"You've known for a month and you didn't think to tell me?"

"I was trying to find out the best way to break it to you. Then when I finally plucked up the courage, you told me about your new girlfriend!"

Heat flooded his cheeks. "She means nothing to me – she's not even my girlfriend –" he said quickly.

"Well, it's none of my business really . . . you can do whatever you want to do now that we've broken up –"

"Lily – please – we went out a couple of times but it's not serious –"

"You don't need to explain – we had broken up – you were ready to move on – I get it!"

"Just listen to me," he said desperately. "I was hurting and I wanted you to hurt too, so I made it sound more than it was, but I'm sorry . . . if I had known you were pregnant – I never would have done that." He lowered his gaze. Silence fell between us.

"So when are you due?" he asked eventually.

"August."

"That's a nice time of year. The baby will be hardy by the time the winter comes."

I nodded. "Look, Sam, I know this is a shock; hell, I still can't believe it myself sometimes except for the fact that if I'm not puking, I'm peeing, but whatever happens between us, I really hope you want to be a part of the baby's life –"

"You're right, this is a big shock for me, Lily. It's huge and I'm still trying to get my head around it all to be honest, but you know how much I've always wanted to be a dad. I want to be there for you – for you and the baby."

"You do?"

"Of course, I do, what do you take me for?"

"Well, I'm glad. No matter what happens between us I want my baby to know its father."

"Lily, I'm here for you, I don't want you to do this on your own. I've only a couple of weeks left in New York, so once I wrap things up, I'll be coming back to Dublin. If I'm going to be a father, I want to make sure I'm involved in our baby's life. I'm going to be there with you every step of the way."

Suddenly, I was overwhelmed by a wave of relief as tears began to stream down my face. "Oh, Sam, I've missed you so much – I love you – I know you might not believe me after everything that has happened between us but I really do. I just wasn't ready for marriage, but I wanted to be with you – I still do."

"You see, I guess I'm different because to me if you love someone, marriage is the next step . . ."

We were going over old ground and it wasn't going to

273

help.

"Look, I've missed you too." He softened. "The last few weeks have been horrendous – you broke my heart."

"I'm sorry, Sam, I love you more than anything, you know that don't you? Please can we try again?"

He shook his head. "I can't –"

I nodded in resignation as all my hopes came crashing down around me again with a thud. "It's okay," I said in a small voice. I was trying so hard to hold back the tears.

"I can't be without you," he continued. "To be honest, you've been on my mind constantly. Unfortunately for me, I still love you, Lily. No matter how much I try to tell myself that I don't or that I'm over you, I'm not. I don't want anyone else. Only you. I've loved from the day I found you picking up all those cupcakes off the floor. Look, I know you probably want nothing more to do with me after how I've treated you but I want to be there for you, every step of the way for the sake of our baby. I want to be the best dad I can be. I'm old-fashioned, I don't want our child to have to split their school holidays or to have one set of clothes in Mum's house and another set in Dad's house – I want us to be a proper family."

My stomach flipped, and I dared not hope. I couldn't believe I had heard him right. "Really?"

He shook his head. "Let's try again – put the past behind us and make a fresh start. What do you say?" He took me into his arms and lifted my chin up towards his, and I found myself melting into his perfect kiss.

CHAPTER 46

I lay blissfully in Sam's arms for the rest of the morning until eventually I couldn't ignore my growling stomach any longer.

"The baby's hungry," I said, stretching. I pulled back the duvet and went to get up.

"Hey, get back there," Sam said. "You're not going anywhere. You're supposed to be resting!"

"But I'm starving!"

"You stay where you are. I'll make you a breakfast that New York would be proud of."

"Can I have bacon and mushrooms . . . and beans – I'd love beans . . . oh, and maybe some scrambled egg too?" My nausea had started to subside in recent days and my appetite had returned in full force just like Frankie had said it would. I couldn't get enough food into me.

Sam cocked his hand against his forehead in mock salute and went out to the kitchen.

I sank back against the pillows with a big smile on my face. I could hear him moving around outside; the noise of the kettle as it came to life, the opening and closing of the fridge door, the pop of the toaster. I felt so much lighter, and I finally realised what a weight I had been carrying around with me for the last few weeks. I couldn't believe what had just happened. I was so happy that Sam was here and that we were going to try again to make a go of it for the sake of our baby. I felt as though I had won the lottery and I was going to do everything I could to make it work this time. Now that I had Sam back I was never going to let him go again.

I was lying there waiting for him to return with my breakfast, but after ten minutes, when he still hadn't come back in to me, I shouted out to him, "I hope you're not sick of me already!"

I was met with silence, so I pulled back the duvet and got out of bed to see where he had gone. I made my way into the kitchen, and I found him sitting on the sofa. His forehead had creased into a deep V between his eyebrows. I looked down and saw in his hands he was holding the copy of *Irish World* magazine.

I felt my stomach somersault and I groaned internally. I had forgotten it was lying on the coffee table. How could I have been so stupid?

"So, when were you going to tell me you made the cover of *Irish World* magazine?" he said, holding it up to me. Hurt and anger filled his eyes.

"It wasn't like that, I swear!" I said quickly.

"Well, that's what it looks like to me! What the hell am I meant to think when I see an actual photo of you kissing Marc?" he roared. "God, I'm such an idiot. I was right all along, you were never over him and you never will be!" He tossed the magazine down onto the table and began pacing the room.

"It was framed to look like a kiss." My voice was panicked. "Marc came into *Baked with Love* and he leaned in to

276

hug me, so I hugged him back. I promise you, that's all it was – just a hug. Dad was there, he saw it all – ask him, I swear I'm telling the truth. The worst part is that I think he might have set the whole thing up himself to earn a bit of cash."

"I don't know, Lily . . ." He shook his head. "Why should I believe you this time? It's just one more thing in a long line of things. Why is your ex-husband still causing so many problems for us? Every time I think we're moving forward, Marc pops up and puts a spanner in the works! I don't want to hear to any more excuses or lies!" He held his head in his hands. "Just a few minutes ago I was so excited that we were able to work it out, and then once again something happens with Marc!"

"You have to believe me, Sam, the only feelings that I have left for Marc are of pure disgust." I paused. "I swear on our baby's life, I'm telling you the truth."

The strength of my words hit home, he lifted his head up and looked me in the eye. "Why should I believe you?"

"Because it's me, we have a history together. Ask Dad – he'll tell you exactly the same thing as I have!"

He whole body slumped down, and he cradled his head in his hands again. "I feel like I'm always in his shadow." His face was crumpled, defeated.

"He means nothing to me. It was you that made me brave enough to trust again. You showed me what it took to love again when I never thought I could. I only want you –"

He shook his head and looked at me squarely. "Will we ever be free of him?"

"We can be, if you trust me. Please, Sam, can we just start

277

again? You have to believe me – I love you and only you. This baby is our future, me and you, we can't let Marc jeopardise that."

He looked agonised.

"Please, Sam –" I reached for his hand. "I want to do it with you. I want you at the scans, I want you there to cut the cord, I want us both to spend hours just staring mesmerised at our sleeping baby in its cradle, but most of all I want you."

"Do you not think I want that too?" He stood up and began pacing around the room. "But things have changed now – it's not just me and you anymore; we can't keep making up and breaking up like teenagers. We have a baby to think of now, we need to get it right –"

I nodded. "I know, but isn't that why we need to give it another shot? I want to share my future with you, Sam."

We looked at each other head on and suddenly all the old hurts, fears, and worries melted away. Sam walked over and took me into his arms. "A fresh start?" he said.

"A fresh start," I whispered back.

Then he lifted my chin upwards and our lips met. We kissed deeply making up for all the distance between us over the last few months. I pulled back from him suddenly. There was one way I could show him for sure the strength of my feelings for him. I knew this was the only man I could ever see myself with and I sure as hell wasn't ever going to let him go again.

"What's wrong?" he said, his face reading confusion.

"Ask me again, Sam."

"Ask you what?"

"To marry you."

He pulled back and his eyebrows shot up. "Are you serious, Lily?"

I nodded before biting down on my bottom lip. "I'm sorry it has taken me until now to be able to say that, but this is what I want, Sam. I want to spend the rest of my life with you – I want to marry you!"

Dark stubble peppered his skin and his kind eyes twinkled. He grinned that smile that I loved so well. "Lily McDermott, will you marry me?"

A bubble of excitement fizzed up inside me. "Yes, a million times, yes!"

EPILOGUE

It was a lovely evening in late spring, sprinkled with the promise of long summer days to come. It had been a busy day earlier, but now *Baked with Love* was quietly awaiting the arrival of the first guests for our engagement party.

"Ready?" Sam asked.

I nodded, and he flicked the switch on the fairy lights that we had hung after the last customer had left. I clapped my hands together gleefully as the whole room lit up magically.

Sam's family were the first to arrive. Marita ran straight over and hugged me. "I'm so glad you two worked it out because I can't wait to be an auntie!" she squealed.

I couldn't help but get caught up by her enthusiasm.

Clara, Tom, and the boys came through the door next. Clara and Tom were holding hands. I was glad to see that the events with Olga were put behind them and if anything they were now more in love than ever.

"Lily!" she sang, kissing the air around my face and grabbing the champagne flute out of my hand before I had a chance to give it to her. She had dressed the boys in miniature suits with bowties. They were tugging at their collars, trying to loosen them, but Clara kept swatting their little hands away.

"So how are my two favourite little men?" I asked the boys while Clara had gone to hang up all their coats.

"You look fat, Auntie Lily," Joshua said.

It had been a few weeks since I had last seen the boys and my bump was starting to push forward, so I suppose I probably did look fat.

"Cheers, Joshua!"

"Er, I'll just see if Clara needs a hand . . ." a mortified Tom said, excusing himself.

"Did you know that your Auntie Lily has a baby in her tummy?" Sam said, crouching down to Joshua's level.

"But she's not married!"

"Well, no, but you don't have to be married to have a baby –" Sam said.

"Yes, you do." He nodded definitely. "My mummy said that."

Sam grinned and leaned in to whisper in my ear. "We had better get up that aisle quickly or you'll have a lot of explaining to do!"

"You'll never guess who I just met –" Clara said, rejoining us.

"Who?" I said.

"Well, I needed change for the parking meter so I went into that new Starbucks and guess who was standing in a black apron asking the queue if they wanted a tall-, grande-, or venti-sized coffee?"

"Who?" we all chorused together.

"Marc!" she said, smacking her lips together triumphantly.

I nearly choked. "Marc – are you sure, Clara?"

"Oh, it was definitely him all right, at first he tried to pretend that he didn't know me, but when I insisted that I knew him, he hissed that he was trying to go incognito and that he was only working there to get into character for his new role!"

We all fell around the place laughing. God, he was pathetic. "I think Nadia finally got tired of bankrolling him."

"That my friend is called karma," Frankie said, giving me a high five.

Dad arrived through the door a few minutes later, but my jaw dropped when I realised that he wasn't on his own, Mabel was standing beside him. He began to blush profusely as all eyes landed on the pair of them. I looked over at Clara who was studying Mabel with narrowed eyes, and I prayed she wasn't going to say anything to ruin it for Dad.

"Dad! Mabel! Here, have a glass of bubbly," I said, mentally telling myself to close my mouth and compose myself.

I risked another glance at Clara, and almost in slow motion, her features began to relax and the crease in her forehead softened. She could see what I could – Dad looked happy. It had been a long time since we had seen him like this. "Mabel," she said, holding out her hand. "It's lovely to meet you."

Once everyone had a glass in hand, Tom raised a toast. "To Lily and Sam!"

"To Lily and Sam!"

A chorus of clinking glasses filled the air. Frankie and I banged our glasses of apple juice together with a wink. I was relieved to see that she was taking much better care of herself. She was going to bed early at night and getting up early in the morning. She had given up alcohol and had joined the gym. She declined invitations to launch parties or nights out because she didn't trust herself yet. I knew it was tough on her when the people she worked with constantly were asking her to come out with them "just for one," particularly after a hectic shoot, but she stayed strong and just made up an excuse about why she couldn't join them. Already she was looking better. Her skin had lost the grey lackluster pallor and puffiness it had taken on in recent months, and she looked more youthful.

"Speech, speech, speech!" Frankie chanted and everyone fell quiet as Sam cleared his throat. "Well, I just want to say thank you to my beautiful fiancée, Lily, for finally agreeing to be my wife. And now that I've finally got her to say yes, I'm going to put a ring on it sharpish before she changes her mind again," Sam said.

There was raucous laughter.

I looked around at my little bakery where the fairy lights twinkled softly. It was filled with the people who meant the most to me. And although Clara was holding her champagne flute up to the light to check for fingermarks, while Tom was swiping a glass from Jacob's hand just before he lowered the champagne down his throat, I felt so blessed. I lay back in Sam's arms and thought to myself how lucky I was to have all of this. I had an amazing boyfriend and we were set to become parents, I had the best friends and family a girl could ask for, and I had a job I loved. When Marc had left me, I thought my world had ended, but in reality it was only beginning, and everything that had come after that had been amazing.

I noticed Dad had put his arm around Mabel's shoulder, and she rested in against him like they had always been together.

I always thought I would find it strange seeing Dad with a girlfriend, but instead I felt happy for them both. They were perfect for each other. I could see that lately Dad had a new joie de vivre about him that I had never seen before and now I knew the reason.

I felt our baby give me a little kick as if to say they wanted to be included in the party too. I placed my hands over my growing bump and let myself soak up this feeling of sheer happiness.

This is the bit where I say "and they all lived happily ever after" and we did. The magic of cake had brought so much happiness into our lives; it had lead me to Sam, it brought Mabel into Dad's life, and Frankie . . . well, right at this moment she is chatting to Sam's friend Harry. There's a sparkle in her eyes that's been missing for a while now, so who knows, maybe cake will work its magic once again?

THE END

If you enjoyed *Baked with Love*, then I would really appreciate if you could help me out by leaving a review on Amazon. Reviews really help to get a book noticed by Amazon who will then promote it to new readers so they are hugely important to us authors. It doesn't have to be long – just one line will do – and I will love you forever. ☺

BAILEYS WHITE CHOCOLATE GATEAU RECIPE

This cake is a real show-stopper, it's rich and decadent and with 3 sponge layers, it's BIG too so would make a perfect celebration cake especially at Christmas for non fruitcake fans. If you're not familiar, Baileys is an Irish cream liqueur made from whiskey and gives a gorgeous flavour to the frosting.

INGREDIENTS

- 300g butter (the real stuff please ☺)!
- 150g white chocolate – use good quality chocolate like Green & Blacks as some brands tend to curdle when you melt them.
- ½ teaspoon vanilla extract
- 5 eggs
- 300g golden caster sugar
- 300g self-raising flour
- ½ teaspoon baking powder
- Splash of Baileys

BAILEYS FROSTING

- Frosting 240g butter
- 120g icing sugar

- 2 tbsp milk/Baileys

METHOD
- Heat the oven to 180c for a fan oven 160c for gas.
- Grease 3 x 20cm sponge tins
- Melt the butter and chocolate together over a medium heat, then pour into a mixer bowl and allow it to cool for 10 minutes. Don't worry if it separates when it cools.
- Beat the butter and chocolate mixture together and then add in the eggs one by one along with batches of the sugar.
- Add the vanilla, flour and baking powder and mix to make a smooth batter before adding a splash of Baileys.
- Pour into the 3 tins and bake for 20-25 minutes. Check by inserting a clean skewer into the centre and if it comes out clean, it's done.
- Allow the cakes to cool and then tip them out of their tins gently onto a wire rack while you make the frosting.

BAILEYS FROSTING
- Mix room temperature butter the icing sugar until it makes a smooth paste.
- Add the liquid if you like a strong Baileys taste you can add 2tbsp but if you prefer subtle, add 1tsbp milk and 1 of Baileys – you can adjust the ratio to your preference. Be careful not to add it altogether, you don't want the

icing to be runny.

- Assemble the cake by sandwiching the layers together using the frosting and then use a spatula to decorate the top and sides. Then finish by grating white chocolate and sprinkle over the cake. Then prepare to wow your family and friends.

-

- Enjoy xx

ACKNOWLEDGEMENTS

This book has been a while in the making and, as is the case in life, lots of things have happened in the meantime, so I want to thank all my loyal readers and people who contacted me wondering when it would be ready – thank you for your patience, I hope it has been worth the wait. I hope you will enjoy seeing what Lily has got up to since.

I wish to thank my ever-present family who put up with endless burnt dinners because I'm off in a fictional world once again.

I also owe a huge thank you to the amazingly supportive blogger community who have been so supportive of The Girl I Was Before. I am always amazed and so grateful for the job that you do helping us authors to spread the word.

I must also thank fellow author Janelle Brooke Harris who has been an invaluable help to me in my writing and is also a great coffee & cocktail date. My fellow bunkerettes – you know who you are – for their encouragement and advice. Najla Qamber (http://www.najlaqamberdesigns.com) for her brilliant cover. Once again you have been a pleasure to work with and can somehow manage to deliver exactly what I want when I don't even know myself. Chrissy from EFC Services for your eagle eye.

Lastly, thank you for reading this book, it never ceases to amaze me that people take the time to read something I created in my head – I have to pinch myself that I get to do this for a living, and I'm very lucky!

Izzy xx

Printed in Great Britain
by Amazon